CHICK
BASSIST

A Lazy Fascist Original

Lazy Fascist Press
An Imprint of Eraserhead Press
205 NE Bryant Street
Portland, Oregon 97211

www.lazyfascistpress.com

ISBN: 978-1-62105-062-9

TABLE OF CONTENTS

Dedicated to the Queen of Rock

CHICK
BASSIST

TRACK 01
DRUMMER OR THE DRUM

Any minute now, you're going to get up off the couch, you're going to grab your keys, and you're going to head out that door. You're going to squint at the sunlight, put on your shades, and start that six-block trek downtown. You're going to stop at The Smoking Monkey, the bar that used to be called Charley's, that bar where you made out with Tish in the men's room that Halloween night after you played that kick ass show. Christ, was that really three years ago? Any minute now, you're going to walk to the bar, you're going to sit down, you're going to have a beer, and when Robbie finally shows up you're going to buy him a beer with the ten bucks that Erin gave you last night. And as he drinks that beer, you're going to let Robbie know that he is now and forevermore officially the *ex*-bass player of Heroes for Goats. You're going to give him the bum's rush, the boot. You're going to do this. You're going to do it because what Robbie did on Saturday night was inexcusable. You're going to do this because, like Erin said, Robbie is unpredictable, a fuckup, an addict, a junkie, and it's only a matter of time before he hurts someone other than himself. You're going to do this because you're the drummer, the heartbeat of the band. You're going to do this.

Any minute now, you think to yourself as you watch the clock hands creep along. You could just say fuck it, pocket Erin's ten bucks, and tell her Robbie never showed. You could just take another pull off the bong and stay home all day, watch cartoons or practice or read old comic books or something. You could get yourself another drink, for courage, for fortitude. No, you've got to do this. You've got to be the one. You promised Erin that you'd take care of things. You saw how he acted toward her, how he pushed her. You can do this. You can take the beating. You can sit there, drink your beer, and listen to whatever lame excuses Robbie throws you. You can just let it flow past you. You can be bulletproof. It's like your dad said after those kids in grade school pushed you into that ditch and broke your sticks: "If you're going to be a drummer, some days you're going to have to be the drum." You're going to do this. You can do this.

Any minute now. Any minute now, you're going to get up off this couch and you're going to forget about the bong on the coffee table. You're going to lace up your boots, grab your leather, and head out that door. You're going to march the six blocks to The Smoking Monkey. You're going to march past the Laundromat where Tish used to buy her dime bags, back before she went clean and found Jesus. You're going to march past Marduk's Liquor Store, past the graffiti-covered out-of-service bus stop with its shattered glass, past the old lady on Fourth Street that always hits you up for spare change. You're not going to blow this off. You're going to head down to the bar, savor your beer, and let Robbie have it with both barrels. Shit, you might as well be going over to his house in the middle of the night to smother him with a pillow. He's not going to take this sitting down. He's going to freak out, yell, throw his beer across the room. He's going to take a swing at you, call you an asshole, a traitor. He's going to make a scene, and Mark behind the bar is going to have to call the cops. You could just blow this off, keep the ten bucks, fire up the bong, and turn on the TV. You could just tell Erin that you forgot, that Robbie never showed, that the bar was closed. You could just start practicing somewhere else across town, change the name of the band, and hope that Robbie never catches on. But no, you can't do that. You gave Erin your word. You said you'd take care of it. You're the drummer. You're the drum. You can take it.

Any minute now, you're going to get up off this couch, pull on your boots, take a quick bong hit for courage, and head out into the unforgiving sunlight to accomplish this dirty deed. You're going to walk through the alleyway where you held Tish's long black hair back out of the firing line as she puked out the ghost of too much partying. You're going to walk past the wall where she spray painted your names entwined in a big black heart, back before she found Jesus and stopped returning your calls. You're going to walk past the burned-out remains of Amsterdam's, the biker bar where the skinheads rioted last summer. You're going to stand out in front of The Smoking Monkey and finish your cigarette. You're going to crush that cigarette out on the sidewalk beneath the sole of your boot, you're going to go inside and order a beer, and you're going to wait for Robbie to show up. You're going to shatter Robbie's dreams, kick his dog, and piss on his cornflakes. You're going to say it just like Erin told you to: Look, Robbie, you fucked up, you need help. You're a junkie, an addict. You're unreliable, you're violent, you're out of the band. Yeah, you can do this.

Any minute now, you're going to stop feeling sorry for yourself, stop thinking about Tish, stop dwelling on the past. You're going to take a hit off the bong that Tish gave you for your birthday two years ago, then try to figure out where you left your boots. You're going to put on your boots, lace them up, grab your leather, your armor, and head down to The Smoking Monkey. You're going to meet Robbie there, and you're going to kick him out of the band. You're not going to sit at home in a stoned stupor thinking about Tish and wondering how she could have left you for a dead guy. You're going to do exactly what you told Erin you would: you're going to meet Robbie at the bar, buy him a beer, and drop the hammer. You're going to tell him that he fucked up, that he crossed the line by shoving Tish, and that he's out of Heroes for Goats for good. You're going to tell him that he needs to clean up his act, that he needs to get help. Any minute now, you're going to walk out that door, walk down to the bar, and Robbie will be waiting there for you. You're going to buy him a beer and tell him that he's out of the band. You're going to listen to his excuses and just let them bounce off of your Teflon skin. After that, you're going to walk home past the apartment where you lived with Tish and try not to think of her. You're going to walk past the vatos working on their lowriders on Fifth Street and try to avoid eye contact. You're going to walk past the skinheads drinking beer out of paper bags on Third Street and try not to say anything stupid. You're going to kick Robbie out of the band, walk home, take a couple of hits off the bong, and watch TV. You can do it. You can take it.

Any minute now. Any minute now, you're going to get up, turn off the TV, put the bong away, put on your boots, grab your leather, grab your keys, and head down to The Smoking Monkey. Robbie is going to meet you there. He'll already be waiting inside. You're going to give him the bad news, that Erin wants him out of the band, that he went too far when he shoved her. You're going to play it cool, buy him a beer with the ten bucks Erin gave you, and let him down as easy as you can. You're going to listen to his sob stories, listen to how he's trying to kick his habit, how he deserves another chance. You're going to let him believe that Erin is the bad guy, that she's the villain, that she's the one who wants him out of the band. You're going to do your best to avoid conflict. You're going to drink your beer, kick Robbie out of the band, and go home. You're not going to sit here on the couch all day debating whether or not you should try to call Tish. Besides, you'd probably just get one of her parents anyway. You're going to do exactly what you told Erin you would: you're going to deal with the situation. You're going to do this because, like Erin said, Robbie is unpredictable, a fuckup, an addict, a junkie, and it's only a matter of time before he hurts someone other than himself. You're going to do this because you're the drummer, the heartbeat of the band. You're going to do this.

Any minute now.

TRACK 02
ANYONE CAN PLAY GUITAR

Erin Locke, the Queen of Rock, wakes up at the crack of noon. "La Cucaracha" has infested her dream, and now echoes through her hotel room. "What the fuck is that?" Erin's voice is muffled by the thick blankets that completely cover her. Beside the lump that is Erin lies a black Ibanez bass guitar. A Heroes for Goats sticker adorns its reflective surface. Erin thrusts one arm out from beneath the blankets and fumbles for the nonexistent alarm clock. She's still slogging off fragments of her dream, that goddamn recurrent creep-out where she's a praying mantis, translucent green, perched on the crest of a burning city, devouring her still-copulating preymate. This time her meal had worn her father's face. Those dreams were the worst. Other nights the dream would feature Paulie's face, or even Lou Reed's. Those times weren't so bad. There was something magical, almost poetic in devouring Lou Reed. One day she'd meet him, the man himself, lure him into a dark alleyway, and there she'd consume him, absorb his power. Fuck. Too quickly, her thoughts shift to Sunday. Sunday she woke up from nightmares of Robbie, wearing her father's face. She woke up crying. This time she was only a little bit hung over. Erin stretches as the dream dissipates, fades from view, but never quite goes away. "Lunchtime," mumbles Erin. "Time to rock and roll." She listens to construction noises across the street, the deaf neighbors shouting at each other, the murmuring television left on last night. *Dracula's Daughter* was on channel twenty-three, but she fell asleep halfway through it. She groans, yawns, stretches, finds the ghetto blaster on the nightstand. Her shoulder still aches. Fucking Robbie.

"White Light/White Heat" [00:00]

She hits "play" on the tape deck. Wheels squeak to life and a chopping guitar beat erupts from the speakers, drowning the outside world and its uninvited noises. She deftly plucks a cigarette, not the lucky one, from its stiff cardboard pack and lights it as it touches her lips in a single fluid motion. Her feet hit the floor. She draws in a lungful of smoke. The carpet crunches slightly. Across the street, a roach coach drives away from a construction site, and workmen start to eat egg-salad sandwiches. Erin exhales. She opens her eyes.

White Light/White Heat, The Velvet Underground's best goddamn record ever, plays for the three hundred and thirty-third time. This tape's been a part of Erin's morning ritual almost every day since the last time she saw Paulie. The tape's A side, *White Light/White Heat*, is followed by five minutes of silence. The B side is *Live at Max's Kansas City*. She's listened to the B side exactly twice. The A side is just too good, worth rewinding for. The tape, like everything in life, deteriorates a little every time she plays it. A few magnetic particles stay behind, the plastic stretches, friction pulls at the wheels. Tiny holes appear. Dropouts. Every time Erin plays the tape, her soundtrack, her memories degrade.

It's still mostly dark in the room, and it takes Erin's eyes a few moments to focus. She must be getting old. Sometimes she's tempted to steal a pair of glasses from the drugstore, granny glasses, just to see if they help. Maybe rose-tinted ones. Yeah, that's it. That's all she needs. Just put on a pair of magical lenses and things will get better. More cash will come in, "A Killing" will get more than local radio, national, maybe even international. She'll find a new bassist. Christian the drummer'll stick around, Christian's loyal to a fault. She can stick it out, stay in town, not let Robbie get the best of her. The rosy shades would make sure of that. She could play some little acoustic things here and there in the meantime. Coffee shops, libraries, busking. She wished she could just play bass herself, maybe she could have herself cloned. That'd be easiest. Besides, she missed playing bass. She could have herself cloned twice and play drums, too. Who needs a band? Heroes for Goats could be a self-sustaining organism.

Eventually, she focuses. A beam of sunlight streaks through the hole in the blackout curtain, paralyzing specks of dust and purple curls of smoke in midair. On the television, a smiling cartoon airplane repeatedly smashes into a building. "Deer in headlights," she yawns, stretches again, reaching toward the ceiling, cigarette perched between two fingers. Erin carefully crushes the burning coal of her half-smoked cigarette in a bedside ashtray, no sense letting it go to waste. She peels off her Motörhead t-shirt and tosses it into the corner with her other clothes, then walks to the bathroom, flipping off the TV on the way.

"The Gift" [02:47]

The tile floor is cold, as is the porcelain toilet seat. Erin pees, listening to its rhythm against the water in the toilet bowl, hits the shower with a vengeance. She doesn't flush first, that would spoil the pressure. Hot water only, not quite scalding. Wonderful. It's been a week since she last washed her hair, and maybe by adding a little bit of water she can make the conditioner go far enough. It always goes twice as fast as the shampoo. In any case, she'll be able to toss the empty bottles, leave them behind. Less crap to carry. As she lathers her hair, Erin thinks about Paulie. Was it a year since she'd seen him? She'd been missing him even before Marco at Zion-I Records called last week. "Erin, hey," came the stranger's voice through the phone. "Look, we're auditioning bass players for Paulie Gray. Paulie mentioned you. Listen, if you can make it up to San Francisco in the next couple of weeks, we'd love to try you out."

This was serious. A real label. The big time. And playing with Paulie again, even if it was just bass. Man, that would be great. Sure, it's a reggae band, but she can fake it. She did just fine back in the day playing Clash covers with Paulie, and those were reggae baselines, she'd do fine now. She thought it funny how Paulie was all serious Rastamon now, she'd always thought of him more white than black, more like his mom than his dad. Suburban. Picket fence. Station wagon. Wonder Bread.

Erin's first band was Paulie's third. Niggers of the Narcissus. Paulie got the title from a book by the guy who wrote *Apocalypse Now*. Paulie read it, she never had. He tried to explain it once or twice, but literature was lost on her, boring. Later, after they heard that someone else had beaten them to the name, they changed it to Self-Absorbed Negro. It seemed only fitting that he'd eventually be fronting The Paulie Gray Band.

At first, Erin and Paulie had played punk rock cover tunes, a few originals, over a drum machine's steady beat. She'd fallen in love, her first real love. Paulie was beautiful, defined without working out, café au lait, dreadlocked. He smelled like cinnamon and sandalwood. They'd have had perfect children. He taught her bass, guitar, music theory, and how to smoke dope out of an apple. "Anyone can play guitar," he'd say when she got frustrated. "Most of rock and roll is just the one-four-five, the tonic, the subdominant, the dominant. Empires have been built on the one-four-five." It was Paulie who first called her the Queen of Rock, and the fact that she turned it into the battle cry that opens up "A Killing" gets her through the day.

Sometimes he could be so smug, so into himself, though. That's why she had to bail, had to make it on her own. She'd grown tired of his quips, his Jimmy Page-isms. "Rock and roll is creative forgery," he'd say. "Steal from the best. When you fuck up and hit the wrong note, do it again. People will think you're improvising." Sure, they spent countless hours on stage or in each other's arms, and watched a thousand monster movies together, and those times were good, but he's just too self-absorbed, too into himself.

As Erin coaxes the last remnants of the conditioner from the bottle into her hand, her thoughts turn to Robbie. She broke a cardinal rule, her rule, by sleeping with him. Sure, it was after a good show, after the label people had been talking to them, and they were both pretty tanked, but she fucked up by giving in. "Hey baby, we did it," he said. That led to kissing, which led to grunting, sweating, and swearing. The beast with two backs. She slept with an employee, with Robbie, for cripes' sake. He wasn't anything she could fall in love with. He did all the things a male was supposed to, but still, the connection, the fusion of souls that should accompany those oh-so-base functions just didn't happen. Robbie was just the bass player.

Besides, after it happened, Robbie got weird. First he got all possessive in public, then once she laid down the law with him and told him it wouldn't happen again, he became withdrawn. She figured he was sliding into old bad habits when he started showing up late for shows and fucking off. Saturday they played a bar show and he was drunk and violent. He shoved her into a wall. Robbie had to go. Erin leans her head back, rinsing Robbie away with the conditioner.

Erin throws aside the curtain. Across from her stands her doppelganger, reflecting through the curling steam. Erin flashes her teeth into a growl, and thrusts her arms out to the sides. The mocking form does likewise. Not bad for twenty-six. She turns, examining her pierced and tattooed skin. A life history, six years of ink, branding, memories reflected. The purple-scaled dragon with its tail curled around her right arm represents strength. The burning skull on her left shoulder, mortality. The twin captive bead rings through her nipples are a souvenir of playing in NYC. The black sun over her navel chakra keeps her emotions in check. She looks at her face. Water drips from her black hair. Minimal wrinkles, great cheekbones. It's your bone structure, contemplates Erin, that's what makes you pretty. It's the scars that make you memorable. She grins at the mirror. Maybe she should blow off rock and roll entirely and take Creepy Mark up on his offer to make her a porn star. How hard could that be? Some pictures, a few videos, and she'd be worshipped by millions. Just like rock and roll, but without all the hard parts. "I'm Erin Locke, the motherfucking Queen of Rock," she scowls at the mirror, "I wake up at the crack of noon." She wraps her hair in a towel and steps out of the shower.

"Lady Godiva's Operation" [11:03]

"Which face today?" Erin asks the mirror as she opens her makeup case. Gloria Holden in *Dracula's Daughter*? Zita Johann in *The Mummy*? No, for today, she'll just be Erin. Eye shadow, liner. No foundation. No rouge. Nordic cheekbones have their advantages. Nothing come-hither, nothing overdone. She carefully applies her eyes, transforming herself into the rock goddess that she knows she is. She brushes out her hair, passing the brush through her raven tangles one hundred times.

Yesterday, Erin gave Christian ten bucks to buy Robbie a ceremonial last drink and kick him out of the band. That left thirty-six. Not enough to pay rent next week. She liked this place, it was clean, well, clean as a hotel can get. People leave her alone, but it's unavoidable, it's time to move on. Besides, the deaf gay guys next door yell at each other all the time. Deaf people are noisy. Thirty-six will probably get the van halfway up the state. It won't leave much for food, a room, or anything else, but she figures she can make San Francisco in a day. The van should make it, the tires aren't too bald, and she has the toolbox in the back. That's the nice thing about having a Volkswagen, you can fix most problems with spare change and bubblegum. Any problems, she can sleep in the van. If she plays for tips along the way at one of the rest stops, sells a CD or two, she may be able to manage the trip in comfort. She runs through the list of people that owe her money. Zilch. Well, there is that indie record store on Main Street, but the owner will probably just offer to mail a check. That's all he ever does. Half the bands in town call him Johnny the Jew. She considers Creepy Mark's offer again. Three hundred bucks for some snapshots would be some quick cash, and the van could definitely handle the short hop to LA.

Erin applies lipstick, blood red, then daubs her lips on a Kleenex. She blows a kiss to her reflection, leaves the bathroom and gets dressed. Black jeans, black boots, Black Sabbath t-shirt. The Queen of Rock is ready to face the world.

"Here She Comes Now" [15:56]

Erin sings along with her favorite song: "Now, if she ever comes now, now..." She packs her things, puts her bass back into its case, gets ready. "If she ever comes now, now..." She leans three guitar cases holding her bass, a black Gibson SG, and a Martin acoustic against the wall by the door. Nearby she stacks two microphone stands with her Kustom amplifier and cabinet. Almost ready to go. "If she ever comes now..." She grabs her gear bag, her cables, her microphones, her pedals. Ready, just like for a show. She throws a milk crate loaded with unused effects, tuners, a TEAC four track, and an old Akai drum machine on top of the speaker cabinet. She gathers up her clothes, black concert shirts and jeans, the few nice things hanging in the closet, and thrusts them into two beat-up black suitcases. She grabs the shoebox full of cassette tapes, every song she's ever loved. She'll call Christian when she gets to where she's headed. She grabs the bag of toiletries from the bathroom and flushes the toilet.

"I Heard Her Call My Name" [17:55]

Now, with everything packed, Erin sits down on the edge of the bed. The dream's residue still lingers on the walls of her brain. So many destinations, so many paths. In a minute or so she'd load the van and head out, destination unknown. It was time to wander, time to throw caution to the wind. Still, there was something that she had to let out. She pulls a red spiral notebook from her gear bag. A Sharpie is clipped to its cover. She pulls the cap from the pen, inhales its acrid odor, and starts to write:

Dracula's Daughter

Some people say
I think and drink too much.
But I always try to stop
before I drain the last drop.

Unlike you, Daddy.

I inherited it all from you,
Roman nose, awkward pose,
and that stare, too intense, too much.

But I'm dealing with it.

Unlike you. Alcoholic, fucked-
up time bomb, waiting for the perfect moment
to let shrapnel fly,
piercing passersby (and me).
Sometimes I can't help myself,

I swear. This time, different, no marks,
no bruises, punctures,
show restraint, don't be greedy,
don't take it all. After all,

I am your flesh, your blood.

Yeah, that might work. Erin jams the notebook back into the bag, zips it closed, and picks it up off the bed. She makes the first of several trips to the van, bursting into the sunlight with new resolve. The feedback and drums swelling from the last moments of "I Heard Her Call My Name" transform into the blistering crunch of "Sister Ray," providing a perfect counterweight to loading the van.

"Sister Ray" [22:31]

The sun stings her eyes, but something about its warmth reassures her, makes her feel like everything will work out for the best. She's thinking how nice it will be to see Paulie. Once the van is loaded, Erin looks around the room one last time, making sure she isn't leaving anything behind. She pulls on her leather jacket and a pair of fingerless black gloves. As "Sister Ray" plays at maximum volume, Erin yanks the cord from the wall, and the ghetto blaster switches over to battery power. Time to hit the road.

TRACK 03
CHICK BASSIST

I love this song. I could die to this song.

Fuck, maybe I am dead. My head hurts. Maybe I'm in Hell and my eternal punishment has to do with some demonic little fucker jabbing a power drill between my eyes. Christ! This fucking headache and—fuck—my right hand feels like it's been hit by a truck, and I can't figure out if I need to throw up or piss. Probably both. Simultaneously. Fuck—oh—fuck it hurts. So I'm in Hell, right? No, they wouldn't be playing Iggy Pop in Hell. Fuck, I love this song. So I'm not dead. Step one completed. Here comes the sixty-four-thousand-dollar question: Where in the name of Electric Fuck am I?

Step two, I'll open up my eyes. Here goes. Ugh. Bad idea. It's fucking bright in here. Carpet's clean, too. No cigarettes, no footprints. This is not my apartment. This is not my truck. Bars always have hardwood floors, and the drunk tank's concrete. Fuck. I'm in someone else's house, and I don't remember how I got here. This isn't good.

Rewind. Christ, I love this song. This song is the reason I met Erin. We were both in the Vinyl Solution, both digging through the buck bin. She was holding up a copy of *New Values*, looking at the record up against the light, checking to see if it was warped. She was fucking beautiful, backlit by the neon sign and a life-sized poster of Sid Vicious.

"Hey," I said. "That's the best fucking record ever made."

"Oh yeah?" she responded. "Is it better than *Lust for Life*?"

"You could just melt away and die to the track that closes out side one."

"The Endless Sea?" She bit her lower lip, like she was really thinking about it.

"That's the one." I moved over next to her and pointed to the title on the cover. She smelled delicious, like a coffee shop, all cigarettes and vanilla. She was dressed in the uniform befitting a punk rock princess: ripped and tight black jeans and a black Ramones t-shirt. Her hair was black; her lips, blood red. I was checking her out, trying to get a read on her.

"I dunno." She held the platter up again, looking through it toward me. "It looks a little warped to me."

I had to seize the opportunity. I moved in close and pointed to the record. "Looks like it's scratched, too. My copy's clean. If you want, we could hook up, if you're into it, and I could play it for you. I could even dub you a copy. I make a mean cup of coffee." Shit. Shit. Shit shit shit shit! I can't believe how badly I fucked that up, oh Christ I fucked that up. Fuck! Okay, rewind. Back to the present tense. Where in the fuck am I? Step three. Sit up. Here goes.

There's a trashcan nearby, one of those hip metal office things, so I grab it and throw up into it. I figure that's the only reason why it would be next to me. Somebody had things ready for me, knew I was going to be sick. Somebody was watching out for me. Maybe I'm dead and in Heaven. That would explain the Iggy Pop. The room is still too bright, a blur, and everything echoes, especially inside the trash can. Something smells like clove cigarettes. Finally, I manage to pull myself up to look around.

There's a couch in the room, and a black-haired girl is sitting on it. She's wearing one of those sheer department-store nightgowns, black, the ones you don't get for your mom at Christmastime, and smoking a clove. She looks glamorous. Soft focus, but everything is out of focus. The whole scene reminds me of the nudie playing cards I stole from a kid at summer camp when I was twelve. I'm still having trouble seeing, but already figure I'm better off than the time I woke up in a "kid's room" in a model home. There would be no scrambling over fences and jumping pools this time. I wonder if I got lucky.

Rewind. Christian told me to meet him at The Smoking Monkey at six o'clock. He didn't show up until after ten. I'd been drinking all night and doing lines with Terrri Terrrors in the bathroom. Fucking Terrri Terrrors, too many Rs for her own good. I knew Terrri in high school, back when she still went by Todd and played basketball with my older brother Kevin. I ran into her again shortly after I started playing out in the scene. She sings for this campy glam-goth band called Occam's Switchblade. We gigged with them a few times. They were constantly partying, doing coke in public, all kinds of crazy shit. A few months back, one of the local music 'zines printed a "separated at birth" shot of Terrri and Erin. They kind of look like sisters if you squint. At least they do their makeup the same way. Erin's civil, but in private she hates Terrri, calls her the competition. I think she's fun.

What happened? Oh, fuck. That's right. That little fucker Christian was there to kick me out. That little punk. I knew it was coming, especially after Erin freaked out and hung up the phone on me. I thought we had a good thing going. Fuck. Fuck fuck fuck fuck fuck. Oh fuck. I look at my hand, and even though it looks like I have three of them, I can see a big gash in the back of it. I cut it on that little fucker's teeth.

Oh fuck.

Fuck. It's not like I even like the guy. We're in a band together, but we don't talk about anything but movies. The kid only likes monster movies, worse than Erin. He was already in the band when I joined. Erin's friend. Still, fuck. I knocked a tooth out. I remember it on the floor. I knocked one of Christian's teeth out. I beat his little corduroys-and-hoodie ass into a corner and knocked out one of his teeth. Fuck.

"Hey there Sleeping Beauty," comes a voice, deep, smoky, soft. "You have a little too much partying last night?"

"Hi," I mumble. I've got no idea who this woman is. I wave limply with my right hand. "My name's Robbie."

"Congratulations. You know your own name. Wanna go for Double Jeopardy and tell me mine?" The voice is familiar, but who?

I start to run through my list of ex-girlfriends. Karen Tober, my first kiss. Monica the math whiz. Psycho Susie. Peggy who was cute at the time but would end up weighing three hundred pounds. Quiet Kim. Danielle from Hell. Bury-me-in-a-Y-shaped-coffin Jenni Steele. Martine who was way too into *Star Trek*. Goth Princess Emily. Hatchet Holly who switched teams—fuck that hurt. That girl with the rabbit ears in Vegas. Meghan the Vegan. Erin Locke. None of them. I'm still drawing a blank when she gets up and walks over. You know that quote about Marilyn Monroe being like "Jello on springs?" It's like that, only blurry with the added visuals of the hangover. It's only after she gets right up to me, takes my face in her hands, and stares into my eyes that I notice the stubble. "Well?"

"Hi Terrri."

"Hi Robbie." She kisses my forehead lightly. "Need a rail?"

"Oh God, yes." That'll help me focus. "Let me go piss first. Where's your bathroom?" Terrri points, and I slowly stand up. It feels like my body is made of broken glass. It takes forever to get to the bathroom, but once I make it there, I shut the door and check myself as I piss. No lipstick on the dipstick. That's a good sign. I finish up, tap off, put myself away, and zip up. I give myself the once-over. I'm still dressed from last night. Black jeans, steel toe boots, black t-shirt, bullet belt. I'm ready for my line, Mr. DeMille. As I wash my hands, I see my face for the first time. My right eye is black, swollen, bruised. A huge gauze pad is taped to my forehead above it. It's saturated with dried blood. No wonder my face hurts.

"Don't fuck with your bandages," comes Terrri's voice from the living room, so I head back out without peeking. I need drugs. She's got four thin lines of coke laid out on a little mirror. Next to the lines is a gold-plated razor blade, like the one on the cover of Judas Priest's *British Steel*, and a length of plastic straw. On the mirror's surface, in red, futuristic letters is the word "Foghat." I sit next to her on the couch. We do the lines, and Terrri pulls the dressing off my forehead. She washes my face with a blue washcloth. It feels good, almost maternal. "How much of last night do you remember?" she asks. "Things were pretty fucked. I think the cops might be looking for you."

"Fuck. What'd I do? I remember hitting Christian."

"Yeah, you beat the hell out of that poor kid. He's going to need surgery, you bad, bad boy." She wags an accusing finger in my direction. "Anyway, you drove off in a huff and crashed your truck into a stoplight. I think you hit the windshield. I pulled you out before the cops showed up, threw you into my car, and drove you here, where you were sober enough to get even more fucked up. We both passed out around sunrise. You snore, by the way."

"Oh yeah? I wouldn't know." Then the big fear hits me. "We didn't, umm...?" I motion from her to me and back again with my hands.

"No, silly," she blushes. "I don't do straight boys unless they ask me to."

"Really?" I wasn't sure exactly who Terrri preferred to do.

"Don't sound so disappointed." She crosses her arms across her chest and does an *I Dream of Jeannie* pout, then smiles. She's girlish, but practiced.

"Huh? No, I'm sorry. I just realized that I'm out of my band."

"You should just ditch the fish and come play for me. I'll get Johnny Rainbow to do keyboards or something."

"Look," I say, "maybe it's a sign. I've been feeling like giving up for months now, ditching this whole fucked-up scene and doing something else. I'm not making it. It's not coming together. I play like a goddamn chick bassist and I'm not getting any better."

She laughs. "You're not all that bad, honey." She brushes the side of my face with the back of her hand. "Johnny Rainbow, now he's a chick bassist." She's right, he's terrible.

"I just don't think it's working for me. I feel like I should do something different, start a new genre of entertainment. I'll call it 'stand-up tragedy.' It'll be me, alone on the cold, empty stage, spilling out my sorrows to an audience of critics for twenty minutes. For a finale, I'll hang myself."

"Make it an auto-erotic strangulation and you've got yourself an agent." She smiles, half-crooked. Like Erin. "Nah, fuck that. Listen, you ever hear of the Sybarite Horses?"

"What's that, a venereal disease or something? A gay thing?"

"No, silly, the Sybarites were ancient Greeks. They were also the height of hedonists, *Lifestyles of the Rich and Famous* if it were hosted by the Marquis De Sade twenty-four-seven. They got this way from having the strongest, best cavalry; on horseback, they were unstoppable. They'd ride out in full dress armor, gold-plated and shit, with big purple feathers on their horses' heads, carrying flags, decked out to the nines. Anyway, they'd hit all the little city-states around, ride in, rob the fuckers blind, then ride back to Sybaris and have a party. They were so into their horses that they even taught them how to dance."

"Wait—dancing horses?"

"Yeah, they taught the horses how to dance." She gets up to demonstrate, doing a bump and grind with her arms raised. I have to remind myself that under that mask of femininity, Terrri is still wearing Todd's genes. I realize that "The Endless Sea" is still playing. It must be on repeat. Terrri continues, "So this went on for years, generations, the Sybarites would ride out, kick ass, then come home and party. As you can imagine, the city-states were getting sick of having their asses handed to them on a regular basis. One day an old, blind poet came to a city called Croton. The poet had just been through Sybaris. He told the tale of the amazing dancing horses of Sybaris, describing them in infinite, colorful detail, which, it just occurred to me, he wouldn't have known a fucking thing about since he's blind and shit, but anyway, the King of the Crotons, Mighty Crotonium—"

"Come on, now you're making shit up."

"No, now I'm getting to the good stuff, so shut the fuck up for a minute." She presses a finger to my lips, holding it there, staring into my eyes, sits back down on the couch next to me. She smells good. Really good. Fuck, If I'm going to do anything with her, I'm going to have to make her shave first. Wait. Nevermind. Did I say that out loud? Terrri is still talking, so I probably didn't.

"So Mighty Crotonium comes up with a plan. That year, when the Sybarites ride up on their horses and start to attack the town, all of the musicians in Croton get up on their roofs and start to play. It's a raucous little dance tune, and all the Sybarite horses start dancing, get all caught up in disco fever, and their riders start falling off and getting trampled."

"No shit?" I ask.

"No shit," she responds. "And that's how the Sybarites got wiped out by the Crotons."

"What's it mean? Don't these kinds of stories always have a moral?"

"I dunno. Does it have to have a moral?"

Fuck, she looks like Erin. It's the hair, the curve of her chin, the stage-light smolder in her eyes. Wait, what am I thinking? Terrri is a guy. That's a fundamental truth I'm not quite prepared to deal with. "A story's got to have a moral. Otherwise, why tell it?"

"Maybe it's 'rock and roll conquers all,'" she suggests, thumping her chest twice and thrusting her hand into the air, throwing the goat. "Maybe it's telling you that you should join my band and tell little Miss Erin Locke the Queen Bitch of Rock to go and fuck her hoity-toity little ponygirl ass. Oooh, I'd spank her so good." She coos this last part, miming a whipping motion.

I think about this for a moment, rubbing my chin. I can't picture it. Erin wouldn't go there and neither should I. The coke has taken the edge off my pain. I'm thinking clearly. Before I go and do something stupid, it'd be a good idea to split and take the twig and berries with me. Maybe find Erin, apologize. "Maybe," I finally say, "but maybe the moral is something else entirely. Maybe it's the Sybarites and their horses. They kept doing the same shit, year in and year out. That's how they got beat. They got too wrapped up in the same song and dance, the same entertainments. They never grew up and moved on."

"Whoa." She holds up her hand. "It's just a story. You think too much. Hey, do you want another line?" She pulls a well-stuffed baggie from between the couch cushions and drops a heavy pinch onto the mirror. She chops it into two slender, fine lines, then picks up the straw and gingerly snorts them both. She hands the mirror to me and stands up. She is backlit, angelic. The curve of her body is accented by the flow of her hair. She is beautiful. She really does look a lot like Erin. She drops the baggie of coke onto the mirror. "I'm going to go clean up, put on my face. You hang out, change the music if you want. This CD has been on all night. Don't blame me, I dig the Igster and all, but leaving it on repeat was entirely your idea. Once I'm ready, we can go get some breakfast, and I'll drop you off at home. I'm serious about having you play for me, by the way."

The song is suddenly huge, big as the world, with backup singers, then just as quickly becomes silent. One. Two. Three. Four. The voice of Iggy Pop, bigger than God, fills the room. "In the endless..." he sings. Five. Six. "Sea." Spoken. Whispered. Synthesizers pull the track back down to nothing. Silence. Pure. Real. The track starts up again, twelve measures of echoing drums give way to Jackie Clark's simplistic bass throb.

"One more time," I say.

Terrri Terrrors smiles, turns and walks toward the bathroom, her ass wiggling as she walks. Total pin-up. Amazing, like Jello on springs. I look down at the Foghat mirror and razor blade. I can't make any life-changing decisions right now. The guitar comes in. Now Iggy. "Oh baby, what a place to be," he croaks, "in the service of the bourgeoisie. Where can my believers be?" Maybe I'll try and talk to Erin later, make things better. "I want to jump into the endless sea." Right now, maybe for the first time in my fucked-up life, I'm the one holding the bag.

INTERLUDE #1

Feeling a bit like Lot's wife, Erin glances back at the burning Volkswagen van, watching the blue-tipped flames cover its rusting metal shell. She remembers reading something about the inherent difficulties of extinguishing a magnesium engine block once it really got going. In a matter of moments, her catalogue of worldly possessions has been reduced to almost nothing: the clothes on her back, her leather jacket, her Ibanez bass guitar in its case, her beat-up ghetto blaster still playing "Sister Ray." Everything else is either ash, or in the process of becoming ash. *Sic transit gloria mundi.*

Erin turns her attention toward the highway, endlessly stretching across the desert landscape. South will take her back home, to Garageland, to pointless gigs, to Robbie and Christian. North, on the other hand, eventually leads to San Francisco, to Paulie Gray, to an uncertain and unexplored future. Erin pulls on her leather jacket, shoulders her guitar case, turns up her music, and starts walking, thumb extended, toward the uncharted horizon.

TRACK 04
MAR

All you ever wanted was to leave a mark on the world when you died. Now you're what's marked. Damaged goods. Two weeks of restless nights spent squaring off against your fractured reflection, fingering your upper jaw, digits chasing your bloated tongue away from that gaping two-tooth hole. Manipulating your swollen crusted lip out of the way to reveal empty tissue balancing somewhere between mend and septic failure. Two weeks. Marked. Two weeks of constant pain, of stolen pills, drugstore whiskey, and self-loathing. Two weeks of spiders building webs against the framework of your drums. You can't even talk right, everything comes out slurred. Must have bit down hard as his fists pummeled your face, must have shattered everything.

You're marked.

XXX

Two teeth, one canine and—shit—what was the other... feline? The pills make it hard to remember. Two teeth. Two weeks. Lost. Damaged. Fucking Robbie Snow. It was supposed to be easy. Too easy. You'd tell Robbie to go and he'd be out, he'd back down, then you and Erin would find a new bass player. Reliable one, not a fuckup like Robbie. Maybe Erin'd even let you call in Tish, let her try out. She played bass, once. But now, two weeks of nothing. No contact. No communication. Erin's gone, split town. Fucking Robbie's fault.

Fucking spoiler, fucking violent fuckup Robbie Snow.

Robbie always was an asshole. Smirking, dishonest junkie fuckup. Easy to hate, the things he said, did. Like first time he met Tish. Your Tish, your precious Tish. "No tits," he sneered. "What do you do with her when you get bored, Christian? Flip her over and pretend she's a boy?"

Tish. Tish. Perfection in a single syllable. Her compact body, her mile-deep eyes. Her sharp inhale as you'd press your face into the warm lotus of her sex. The sweet scent of her sweat against your skin. You'd watch her sleep, television turned to a dead channel, watching snow flicker animate the ice blue highways bustling beneath the pale translucence of her skin. A day won't pass when you don't pronounce her name, wishing, regretting. Tish.

Tish, whose favorite band in high school was Guns N' Roses. Tish, who always looked so pure in bonglight. Those first few months when all you did was get high and fuck. Tish, your Tish. Gone. A year and it still aches. Could she love you even now, marked, disfigured? Could she touch your wounded face, reassure, comfort you? Or would she simply gag, disgusted by your altered face? Would she chastise you for not trusting in her god? "You're such a fucking irony, Christian," she said, last time you saw her. "Name like yours, you should, but you don't believe in anything."

But you do believe in something, at least you did. A belief that you would make your mark upon the world. A mark, your mark, like the marks on Tish's body. The black birthday star you gave her, inked into the back of her neck. You'd trace it with an index finger, kiss its raised surface. The welts your nails drew upon her back. The thumbprint bruises you'd leave on her arms after a night of rough animal coupling. That night she took a blade and scratched letters into the skin across her meager belly, "It's your name, Christian, see, I've carved your name." *Tish*, you say, *I'm sorry, Tish*. But you're the one who's marked.

Tish, her name a cymbal crash. You close your eyes, you can still taste her probing tongue in your mouth. *Stay away from the missing teeth*. You can still smell the pungent scent of her sex on your fingertips.

A fistful of pills washed down in a swig of whiskey makes it easier to imagine. You lie on the floor, envisioning her cool blue ghost mounting you, touching you, stroking your face with long black tendrils of hair. Her legs entwine with yours, blurring the line where your body stops and hers begins. You roll your hips beneath her weightless shade, then, embarrassed by the shameless pantomime, curl into a fetal position, jaw throbbing, sobbing. *Tish*, you cry, *I'm sorry, Tish*.

XXX

Eons, days, or moments pass. It doesn't matter which. The dirty tile floor chills your bare skin, peppering you with puckered goosebumps. You pull your knees against your chest, holding tight as geologic periods pass, as suns wink out, as Earth cools to a cinder. Dying creation spins, a bathtub drained. Your stomach tightens, rumbles, evacuates. You heave. Your wounded maw gives birth to a constellation of whiskey and bile, half-dissolved morphine stars and bloodred flecks within. Primordial conception bubbles. Idiot ancestors, blind gods, and superstitious zygotes flail, clash, and crumble. You lie on the floor, embodying the forgotten drifting deity who, drunk on power and new wine, vomited forth the universe.

Eventually the rosy-fingered sun returns, streaming in through the bathroom window, chasing dreams away into dark corners, banishing ghosts. The twin pains, your empty soul, your face, fade to background static. You say her name once more, pronouncing it, a ward against the darkness. You struggle to your feet, unsteady, but resolved. An insect voice murmurs deep within your head: *You may be marked, but you will make your mark*. You grimace at your reflection in the broken mirror, the empty black hole in your face threatening to crush the world in its enormous gravity. *You will make your mark*, you promise. On Tish, on Robbie Snow, on the entire world.

TRACK 05
LIKE A LEPER MESSIAH

They'd fucked to *Ziggy Stardust*, to the B side, the best side, but now she watched him as he slept, a childlike smile splashed across his face. She smoked a cigarette and whisper-sang along with "Rock 'n' Roll Suicide." Between drags, she explored his silhouette with manicured fingertips, realizing only now how much he resembled a long-haired version of his older brother. As the final chord rang to decay, the needle began to scratch the endless circle of the record's lead-out ring. She crushed her cigarette into the stolen hotel ashtray on the floor next to her mattress, leaving a slender lipstick-stained monolith among the many filterbones, the long night's fallen soldiers. She yawned, then got out of bed and walked naked to the bathroom, enjoying the simple pleasure of the thick carpet beneath her feet. Without switching on the light, she sat down on the cold porcelain seat, pressed two fingers against her cock to aim, and pissed into the bowl.

While Robbie slept, riding out in dreams the dregs of last night's cocaine binge, the phonograph robotically lifted its arm, returned it to the vinyl's sharp carbon black edge, expertly slid its needle back into the groove. "Lady Stardust" once again began to play. Terrri, however, paid it no mind. Instead, she remained seated on the toilet, silently contemplating the convoluted ins and outs of sex, and love, and rock and roll in this great modern age.

The last few weeks had been a wondrous blur of mania and music and all the rush and tumble of a new and unanticipated relationship.

She hadn't expected anything when she brought Robbie home from the bar that night. She was just doing a brother a favor, saving his ass before the cops showed up. But then he kissed her, and the strings kicked in. It was only a spontaneous afterthought that prompted her to offer him a place playing bass in her band. Now not only did he have all of the old songs down, but he and Devlin Deck and Johnny Rainbow had already pieced together a dozen brand new melodies to fit her lyrics. Everybody was excited about hitting the studio next month so Occam's Switchblade could start recording their new record. Johnny was pleased as punch to be back behind his precious keyboards, and even though Maxxy Blue at first complained about Terrri's penchant for bringing home "stray dogs," he fell into line and was knocking out a beat on his drums before Robbie struck his third note.

So far, Terrri had confided only to Robbie that her grand plan was that the new record should be a rock opera, tentatively titled *Goddammned Mother Fucker*. He liked the title, but didn't seem to get it when she explained that it would be *Oedipus Rex* retold from Jocasta's point of view, so she ended up telling him the whole story over a fifth of cheap scotch. By the time they killed the bottle, Robbie had apparently decided that "Oedipus, motherfucker" was his favorite thing to say in the whole world. Okay, so maybe Robbie was just a little bit dense. At least he made up for it by being pretty.

Terrri tapped, stood up and flushed the toilet. She walked back to the bed, glanced down at Robbie, watching his eyes flicker behind their lids in the lurking half-light that leaked through the curtains from outside, limning the objects in the room. She wondered what he might be dreaming of. Was it her? Was it someone else? A girl? A boy? Terrri plucked a cigarette from the pack perched atop her nightstand then strolled across the bedroom toward the record player, a practiced nightclub walk that perfectly offset the curves of her slender, feminine body. Her ass-length black hair caressed and brushed the tribal tramp-stamp tattooed valley at the small of her back. Her sculpted breasts swayed slightly in counterpoint to her rounded hips. Were it not for that one thing, that one, little, insignificant thing, then she would pass, completely, for a natural-born woman.

One day, mused Terrri as she lit her cigarette, that final artifact that betrayed her origins as a boy named Todd would finally be gone. She recalled the first time she'd tried on those gold brocade Chinese pajamas from her sister's dress-up box. "What do you want to be when you grow up, Todd?" asked Auntie Drew. "Pretty," answered Terrri. One day Terrri would move beyond this *anima sola* limbo, this hybrid purgatory, an amber-trapped life between the genders. But would she miss it?

That was Terrri's biggest question. After all, her relationship with her phallus had always been a complicated one. It had a habit of getting her into trouble, inspiring her reckless behavior and cocky attitude. No matter how she tried to tuck it back, hide it from the world, it still had a nasty habit of making itself known. Even so, it was a part of her identity and form... for now. Like a leper messiah, she thought. At times, she pictured her body in terms of Eliphas Lévi's etching of the Gnostic goat god Baphomet, hermaphroditic, simultaneously male and female. It was Veronika Vale, Terrri's ex-grrlfriend, the first after she began her transition, who suggested this satanic similarity: "Great tits, long hair, and a nice, hard cock—what more could a grrl want?" Terrri wondered what the last few years had done to shape that angry, sweet, excruciating grrl. Had she finally found her place in the world, or had she just exploded?

She thought of Kevin, too. Robbie's brother. Of the time they'd high-fived one another over Rachael Rimsky's back. No, that was high school, so that wasn't Terrri, that was Todd. But Terrri was the one who, two weeks later, sucked off Kevin in the locker room while the rest of the team played the boys from St. Sebastian's. Poor Kevin, Terrri hadn't just blown him, she'd blown his mind. He was never quite the same after that, and their friendship drifted apart. She did end up receiving an invitation to Kevin and Rachael's wedding, but two days before the ceremony happened and addressed to Todd. By that time she was Terrri full-time, so she didn't bother showing up.

Terrri sat down, cross-legged in front of the record shelf, and fingered her way through the cardstock jackets with her left hand. *Blind Faith, Diamond Dogs, Love it to Death, Love's Secret Domain, Frankenchrist, Appetite for Destruction, Ritual de lo Habitual, Sticky Fingers, Virgin Killer*. Every record seemed to hold a phallic agenda. She took a pensive pull from the cigarette perched between her right index and middle fingers, then exhaled, blowing out a perfect ring, a halo, and watched it ascend and dissipate. Terrri smiled, transferred the cigarette to her mouth, where she clutched it tight between her white and gleaming teeth.

As "Rock 'n' Roll Suicide" once again began to play, she pulled the empty record jacket from the shelf: David Bowie's *The Rise and Fall of Ziggy Stardust and the Spiders from Mars*. She turned it over, and over again, in her hands, examining it. RCA AYL1-3843. "A Gem Production." That mysterious brick building. Those boots, that haircut, that tight blue jumpsuit, sexy circa 1972. That strange English phonebooth on the back, shades of Doctor Who. "To be played at maximum volume," indeed.

INTERLUDE #2

Don't get me wrong, I love The Kinks.

Seriously. When Ray and Dave Davies weren't pummeling each other, they rocked. When they were, on the other hand, they rocked even harder. Nothing quite like brotherly love to make your jaw ache. Still, *that* song, no matter how catchy the fucking thing might be, no matter how much you want to sing along by the end of the damn thing, doesn't quite do the subject justice.

I mean Ray's got it right on more than a few levels. Girls will be boys and boys will be girls. This is a mixed-up, muddled-up, fucked-up world, and sometimes, when I've had just enough, champagne starts to taste like cherry cola (c-o-l-a cola). Thing is, Ray quits telling the story right when it starts to get good. He cops out before it's time to spill the gory details. Who fucks who? Who sticks what where? Who gets to sleep in the wet spot? It's like one of those crappy old movies where the bedroom door swings shut and the audience is left to fantasize that Doris Day is yanking on Rock Hudson's hair, screaming "take it all, bitch" as she fucks him from behind with a big black dildo. It's catchy, but not quite true.

Lola ain't got nothing on Terrri Terrrors.

After all, Lola's just a garden variety transvestite. A weekend faggot that gets his freak on by tarting up in a dress, smearing on a little bit of rouge, lipstick, and fucking with drunk hayseeds, scaring the bejesus out of them. "I'm gonna make you a man." By the end of the night, Ray's got it coming. All the hints are there—the dark brown voice, the crushing bearhug—and no matter how drunk a guy is, he knows the chick's going

30

to turn out to be either a coyote or a cocksucker. The whole thing's just a buildup to the big gag anyway, a chaste one, too, stacked against the raunchy riff from "You Really Got Me." The panties drop and suddenly—sproing!—up it pops like a jack-in-the-box. Shock value, that's all.

But Terrri?

Terrri's something else entirely. She's no reject from the New York Dolls, but a real, live girl—with one exception. She moves like a chick, smells like a chick. She's a chick. My type, even, with black hair, smooth skin, great mouth. Tits to sink a battleship. She's got the rock goddess thing nailed. Like Erin...

...with a penis.

But not a scary one. Not elephantine huge, swinging from knee to knee. No freaky veins, either. Normal. And apparently I don't have any problem with that. Everything worked. Who knew? I can get it up for a chick with a dick, have a great time at it, and not even feel bad about it in the morning. That doesn't make me a fag or anything, does it?

I thought it might, that first afternoon. Terrri'd split, leaving me stoned and alone at her pad, saying she'd be back in an hour or two with breakfast. I entertained myself by digging through her porno tapes. She has a ton of them: straight, gay, bi, trans, something for everybody. Half the time I spent goofing on the titles. I tried watching something called *Rock Hard*, but it just seemed stupid. No reaction. *Fluff Boys* was even worse. I couldn't talk myself into *T-Girl Surprise*. I eventually managed to rub one over a scene in something called *Naughty Nymphs Nine*, a generic blonde in a cheerleader's uniform, nice tits, staring right into the camera as she played the confident fellatrix to a locker room full of swinging phalli.

That did it. Took me ten minutes, tops. The gay stuff didn't even get a rise. Hell, I can't even jerk off in front of a mirror. Dicks don't do it for me.

But Terrri? I dig her. She's a cool chick. I'll admit it weirded me out the first couple of times she jabbed me in the leg while we were going at it, but I can work around it. Throw in the whole band thing, and I've got the perfect girl...

...with a penis.

TRACK 06
YOU GOTTA ADMIT,
THAT'S A NICE SET OF DRUMS

The kid sits on the rail overlooking the freeway, as it stretches down into the valley, dangling his army-surplus monkey-boots over the edge. He steadies himself with his left hand, fingers wrapped around the Suicide Prevention Hotline signpost next to him. In his right hand, with the savant dexterity you've only seen in drummers and idiots, the kid holds the brown paper bottlebag, clutching the exposed smoke-glass neck in the okay-round between thumb and forefinger, and an unfiltered cigarette, tucked in between his middle and ring fingers. He alternates between these two—hit, drink, puff, drink—tunelessly singing along his nonsense cadence to the streaking carlights speeding past below. He hears you approach, soft footfalls against dusk-damp sidewalk. He glances back. "'Sappenin', soul fly?" His voice is malt-liquor-slowed, sibilant, sliding along. "You got another one of those pills?"

You fish in your pocket, reeling in a handful of painkillers: one white with a red cross, two pale green, three light blue with a dark blue stripe. You can't differentiate the colors under the yellow filter of sodium vapor lights, but you've found the patterns make identification easy. You return the blue pills to your pocket, saving them for when you need to shut down, hand one of the greens to the kid. You pop the red cross and the other green into your mouth, followed by a swig from your own bottlebag. You swish the two pills back and forth between the gap in your teeth three times before swallowing them down. The kid pops his pill into his mouth, washes it down with the rest of his beer. He hits the cigarette one last time, drops the glowing butt down the neck of his bottle. He holds his hand aloft, calls "five," rockets the bottle down into the midst of the late commute traffic. The bottle explodes on impact, sending glass and cigarette spark and weasel-piss-coated shrapnel everywhere. Cars screech as they swerve and crunch through glass, grinding it back into sand in a matter of seconds.

"Fuck you, freeway fuckers," yells the kid at the indifferent cars. "The fuck outta Garageland."

The kid plays drums for a band called Sinister Without Smiles. Postpunk trio, tuned to D to make up for their undropped balls. You've been hanging out with them for a couple of weeks now, teching the kid's kit for beer, sitting in for him when he's swiped too many of your pain pills. The kid's new to the band, answered an ad, replaced the band's drum machine, which they sold off to those Nazi faggot fucks in Shithaüs.

The kid lives alone. No real friends, just the guys in the band. Keeps his drums at the practice space. You gotta admit, that's a nice set of drums.

"Loyal to your patch of dirt," you say, setting your bottle on the rail and resting your hands against it. You look over the edge. The cars have already resumed their standard-issue crawl. "You missed."

"Fuckers," mutters the kid. "Commuter sheep. Fuck 'em."

You hock and spit over the edge, hitting the windshield of a speeding truck, which disappears into the valley. "Yeah, fuck 'em."

The kid lights another cigarette and you bum one, along with his lighter, a Chinese-made Zippo knockoff emblazoned with a gold-toned skull. They're cheap ones, the cigarettes, generics, and on your first drag, loose tobacco falls out and sticks to your lips. It takes a few twists and taps between hits, but eventually you improvise a method that prevents it from happening again.

"Garageland?" says the kid. He picks up your bottle and takes a swig, sets it down again. "Land of ten thousand shit bands competing over a dozen-and-one shit clubs." He points north, to an overpass crossing the freeway on the other side of the valley, then drags his finger left a few degrees. "See that green glow up there? That's Immaculate Sacred Heart Hospital. I was born there." He drags his finger a little farther out to the left. "Bright white, next to it? Football field where I went to high school. They must have a game tonight, but I never went to one. Fighting fucking Crusaders. Let's see, I've lived there, there, there, there, and there." He points to each "there" as he annunciates it, an impressive arc across the valley, west to east, spanning the entire twinkling horizon.

He moves his finger back to the starting "there." "In the neighborhood where I grew up, there were four basic houses, set in an endless, repeating pattern. Follow the street all the way down to the cul-de-sac, and you could count them, like tapping out a four-four beat. Sure, there were minor variations, three possible colors—gray, green, blue—and the occasional bay window, dormer, y'know. But when you went to a friend's house, you knew how the layout went: The front door led through the living room, the living room to the kitchen, downstairs was the family room and garage, upstairs, the bathroom, the bedrooms. First ten years of my life, I thought every neighborhood in the world looked like that.

"When I was ten, I started exploring, meeting other kids, at school, shit like that. I figured out that a block or so in any direction, you'd start to hit apartments, neighborhoods with liquor stores, check-cashing joints. That's where the kids with only one parent lived, where the mixed-race kids lived." He picks up your bottle and takes another pull, draining it, then launches it down toward the freeway. It explodes on impact, like the first, again sending cars scattering to avoid the glass shrapnel.

"You know what Garageland is?" He turns to you, points, taking his left hand from the pole and resting it on his knee. "It's roach-infested practice spaces in storage parks, endless freeways, graffitied neighborhoods. Garageland is rootless, pre-planned, prefabricated. It's a piece of shit, but it's my piece of shit." He leans forward, tottering on the edge of the railing. "You hear me, freeway fuckers?" he yells. "I'm the king of Garageland, grand duke of shit town."

The kid is boring you. You wonder if anybody would miss him if you just reached out and pushed. He'd fall, bounce off some commuter's hood, maybe break a windshield. Would they even stop driving? Cops would write him off, just another drunk asshole, not even worth the paperwork. You'd just replace him in the band, they wouldn't even ask about him. One push, that's all it would take.

You gotta admit, that's a nice set of drums.

TRACK 07
SYMPATHY

Over the din of wind, a voice comes. "Hey girl," it shouts, feminine, thin, and childlike. "You need a ride?"

Erin opens her eyes and looks up, startled. She hadn't heard anybody pull up, sitting there at the side of the road with her head in her hands, but there it is in the glinting gravel, a black limousine, all crisp, European lines and blue-black, expressionless windows. Hanging half out of its sunroof is a platinum blonde, her hair a splendid nimbus illuminated by the noontime sun, waving. "Yeah," Erin calls, squinting one eye and holding up a hand to block the bright and unforgiving light. It's a girl, my Lord, Erin thinks, lyrics surfacing from the engraved grooves of her mind as they often do, but then remembers that she hates that song.

"How far are you headed?" shouts Erin. She stands up, dusts off her legs, the seat of her jeans, cups both hands above her eyes blocking the sun. Beside her, the batteries in the tape deck finally begin to die, stretching out the notes, dragging down the pitch of Lou Reed's voice a few cents, a semitone, an octave. Erin reaches down and presses stop, then throws her leather jacket over one shoulder, picks up the tape deck and guitar case from the sun-cracked ground, and feels the burn of hot plastic handles against her hands.

"San Francisco," shouts the girl. "You?"

"Same."

"Great." She punches a fist into the air triumphantly. "I'm bored. Get in."

The girl drops back through the sunroof, as Erin approaches the car and the driver's side door swings open. A tall black man in a black suit glides out, steps around the front of the car, opens a rear door, and beckons Erin inside. His skin is several degrees darker than his suit, his arms too long for the sleeves. He smiles, sharp white teeth gleaming. Dark yellow eyes stand out against a night-black complexion. Inside the plush-upholstered car, the platinum blonde pats the seat beside her. "Come on, sit down. I won't bite."

Erin slides her guitar case and stereo onto the floor, then ducks through the door and scoots across the leather seat until she's right next to the blonde. The driver shuts the door behind her with a resounding thud. For half a second, the world goes dark, and Erin feels her heartbeat pick up tempo, but soon her eyes begin to adjust to the cool and calming shade of the limo's interior. She listens as the man's feet crunch through gravel toward the back of the car, across the back, and up the roadward side. She hears the driver's door slam, the engine start. Blue-tinted lights flicker on, illuminating the passenger cabin with a haunting glow. The blonde, bent over a small mirror and wood grain bar, smiles. "Mix you a drink?" she asks, already dropping ice into a glass.

"Sure," says Erin.

"Whatcha want?" asks the blonde.

"Surprise me." The limo grinds gravel, lurches as it pulls out onto the highway and music begins to play, a familiar shimmying samba voodoo backbeat on a single drum, then congas, a maraca. The blonde presses an icy glass into Erin's hand as a short, bestial yelp leaps from the speakers, echoing across the sparse jungle soundscape. Electric bass and piano join, the bass up front, leading. "Hi, I'm—" starts Erin.

"Shhh..." says the blonde, holding a long, French-manicured finger in front of her pouting lipsticked lips as the singer's howls turn to primitive grunts. "I fucking love this song."

The blonde sings along, a school choir voice, untrained but well in key. Erin joins in on the choruses and the who-who's, but otherwise sits back smiling, entertained by the blonde's performance, sizing her up.

The blonde is pale, clean, and smells like spicy, expensive perfume. Her dress is bright red, thin-strapped, short, low-cut, a size or two too small. Her ample tits press against the dress's restraint, threaten to leap out. Her arms and shoulders are toned, her legs shapely. No visible tattoos. Her makeup is understated yet glamorous, save for a thin black line traced around her blood red lips. Her tongue dances among her small, endearingly misaligned teeth as she sings. The blonde is barefoot, a pair of strapped spike heels kicked off nearby on the floor. She has matching thumb-sized marks bruised onto her biceps. On her left wrist, she wears a blue Velcro and elastic splint. There's something familiar about her, thinks Erin. An actress? A model? One of those girls on the TV that turns the letters?

Erin looks around. Outside, the world speeds past, its blur distorted by the dark-tinted windows. A pane of similar tinted glass separates them from the driver. For a second, Erin thinks she sees his yellow eyes reflected in the rear-view mirror, staring at her. The song ends and the blonde applauds, laughing. She reaches forward with her index finger, pressing a hidden switch on a black panel and interrupting a bluesy acoustic guitar introduction mid-chord. "We fucking rock," she says, taking a drink. "I know who you are now," she says, pointing for emphasis. "I figured it out while we were singing together."

"Oh, yeah?" says Erin, cautiously.

"Yeah. You're in Heroes for Goats. I saw you guys play at Brandon Rigby's Halloween party. I've got your record. Your name's Erin Lake."

"Locke," corrects Erin. She grins. "The Queen..."

"...of Rock. I wake up at the *fucking* crack of noon," the blonde finishes, emphasis placed squarely on the ad-libbed "fucking," displaying erect middle fingers as accompaniment. "Gawd, I fucking love that song, so fucking hot. I use it in my stage routine. I knew it was you under all that dirt! I hope you don't mind me asking, your majesty," the blonde continues, winking. "What in the holy heck were you doing out there?"

"Walking."

"No shit? Looked like you were sitting. You looked lost. I felt sorry for you."

"No shit," says Erin, nonchalant.

"No shit. We saw what was left of a Volkswagen van way back, 'bout twenty minutes before we picked you up. Torched. Cops everywhere. Yours?"

"Yeah," replies Erin.

"That sucks. Lose much?"

"Only everything."

"Oh. At least it wasn't everything."

"Yeah. Good point." Erin takes a long pull from her glass. The alcohol burns the back of her throat, but the liquid is refreshing. Vodka, the good stuff, and citrus, and lots of ice. They ride along in silence for a few minutes, nursing their drinks. Erin mentally catalogues everything lost in the van, assigning each item an arbitrary sentimental value on a scale of one to ten. The blonde is right, she decides. "At least it wasn't everything."

"See," says the blonde, raising her glass as if for a toast. Erin reciprocates, and the two clink glasses. "To everything," says the blonde.

"To everything," answers Erin, draining her glass, crunching a final piece of ice between her teeth. She holds the empty glass aloft between two fingers. "I think I've killed it."

"Refill?" asks the blonde, emptying her own glass.

"If you're having another."

"Of course. Same thing?"

"Surprise me," answers Erin. The blonde turns to start mixing, and Erin glances out the window at the vast expanse of nothingness that spills off into the distance. Tumbleweeds. Crows. Telephone poles.

"Here, try this," says the blonde. "Let me know if that's strong enough for you."

Erin accepts the glass and takes a sip. A ribbon of sweet has joined the previous beverage's sour, tart perfection. Erin licks her lips. "You've got me at a disadvantage," she says. "You know who I am. I don't even know your name."

The blonde shifts her own glass from right hand to left, then holds her right forward in greeting. "Please allow me to introduce myself," she begins, grinning. "Candy Snowdrop, star of sinful stage and screen."

"What?" Erin chuckles, chokes, coughs.

"Candy Snowdrop. That's my handle. My name," says the blonde, defensive.

"Sorry," says Erin, stifling her laugh. "It's just that it sounds like a porn star name."

"Duh," says the blonde, moving her right hand to her hip. "Do I look like a goddamned tax accountant?"

"Geez, no," says Erin. "No offense. I just wasn't expecting...."

"It's cool. What do you say to a porn star, right? What do you say to a rock star?" Candy holds her hand out again. "Hey Rock Star, meet Porn Star."

Erin takes Candy's hand in hers and shakes it. "Pleased to meet you."

"Hope you guessed my name," laughs Candy.

The limo drives on.

XXX

"Why are you heading to the City?" asks Erin, cradling a refreshed drink in both her hands.

"Big party," answers Candy. "Industry people, rock and roll people, pretty people, people who like to watch pretty people fuck. We'll have fun. I might film a scene or two while I'm up, depending on what happens." She holds up her splinted left wrist. "Somebody will probably want to catch this on video. Couple of years ago, I did a picture with a black eye after I fell off my skateboard." She points at her left eye. "It's still my biggest seller. Who knows? Specialty market. How about you?"

"New band, I guess. I'll call an old friend when I get there. I guess I'll find out the details then."

"No kidding? You guys broke up? Shit. You were good. Does that make my record a collector's item?"

"I guess so," responds Erin, glancing down at her dusty boots. "Shit happened. Look, I don't think I really want to talk about it."

"That's cool," grins Candy. "We could talk about me."

The limo drives on.

XXX

Candy fingers the invisible buttons on the smooth black panel, quickly moving from earnest acoustic guitar to flitting violin to nervous talk to methamphetamine electro-pop. Finally she settles on a low, droning hum. "There we go," she says. "Must be the sacred cosmic Ohm station. Will that work for background noise?" She draws up her knees, rests her wrists against them, palms up, and glances skyward, holding the pose only for a moment before laughing.

"I guess so," says Erin, yawning. The road has been long and the drinks potent. "Your name, is it real?"

"Real as you need it to be, just like everything else in my line. Candy's sweet. Everybody wants candy," she pouted. "Angie Macalister, not so much."

"Understood," answers Erin. "Say, Candy. You got a cigarette?"

Candy looks around. "Not back here. Hang on." She leans forward, taps on the glass separating them from the driver's compartment. The window slowly descends. The driver glances at them in the rear-view mirror. "Got any smokes?" asks Candy.

The driver leans to his right and opens the unseen glove compartment, hands back a rumpled red-and-white cardboard package. As Candy takes it, the window ascends, isolating them once again. Candy opens the box. "Only one," she says. "We'll get more when Mubarak stops for gas. Mind sharing?"

"Guess not," replies Erin.

Candy flicks the cigarette into her left hand, places it in her mouth, then presses yet another invisible control near those of the stereo. An unseen door opens. She presses a small plastic handle, waits a few seconds for it to pop back out, raises the glowing coil and lights

41

the white paper cylinder perched between her lips. She takes a drag, French-inhaling a plume of smoke as she takes the cigarette between top knuckles of her slim index and middle fingers, hands it off to Erin. A contoured print of her lipstick marks the filter.

Erin takes the cigarette between thumb and forefinger, shielding it with her remaining fingers, discretely takes a draw of her own. The twin tastes of fine-blended Turkish tobacco and rose-infused lipstick wax ramble over her tongue, filling her mouth, her throat, her lungs. She hands the cigarette back to Candy, purses her lips into an elegant "o" and puffs a pair of smoke rings into the air. They levitate, expand, blur into a lazy eight, then dissipate. "That was cool," remarks Candy.

"One of my parlor tricks," answers Erin.

"I've got to learn that one," states Candy, taking another drag and offering the cigarette to Erin.

"It's all in the tongue," says Erin, accepting.

XXX

Erin rests her head in Candy's lap as Candy sings along with an unfamiliar fifties song she's excavated from the radio. As she sings, Candy strokes Erin's hair. The song's lyrics involve a girl, a boy, a fast car, and a horrible crash. Erin's not really paying attention, instead exploring the soft-edged realm between inebriation and sleep. Soon, she drifts off, begins to snore softly. "There, there," says Candy. "All is safe inside my magic chariot."

But all is not so safe inside of Erin's head. As the waves of sleep roll over her, she finds herself returned to the ever-burning city, standing, pressed up against a bullet-chipped stone wall, breathing heavily in the hot, sulfurous air.

Erin glances down at her hands. In one she clutches a crude knife, the blade formed from a piece of hammered metal, the handle, a broken guitar neck. Both hands have blood on them, but Erin doesn't think it's hers.

"She went this way," calls a gruff, male voice. It has an angered, injured quality. "Bring the chains." Erin feels her pulse quicken, listens to the sound of manly boots on rubble, dogs, the clink of metal on metal. She crouches, holding the knife ahead of her, listens to her own nervous breath as strobing shadows approach...

XXX

"Hey, wake up, sleepyhead," says Candy, shaking Erin. "No time for dreamland. We've stopped for gas. Let's hit up the minimart." Candy climbs over Erin, pushes open the door and the car is flooded with harsh setting sunlight. Erin clambers out behind her, shielding her eyes from the sun. She stretches with a yawn, then follows the equine clop-clop of Candy's high heels into the truck stop's garish convenience store, where a handwritten sign promises "pizza burritos & more."

Candy grabs a plastic basket from a dusty rack beside the door, walks to a glass case, grabs a foil-wrapped burrito, and drops it into the basket. She turns to look at Erin. "You want a burrito or a burger?"

"Neither," says Erin. "What else have they got?"

Candy looks through the case. "Let's see. Egg salad, Turkey and Swiss, Ham and cheese—but that one looks like it's growing—boiled eggs with slices of cheese and saltines, chicken burgers, carrots in murky water." She closes one eye and sticks out her tongue, making an "ick" face.

Erin smiles, nothing sounds good. "How long was I crashed?" asks Erin. She thrusts her hand into an empty front pocket and digs around.

"Couple of hours. Don't worry, I've got it."

"Thanks," says Erin, pulling her hand from her pocket. "I'm tapped."

"Just leave it to your fairy-fucking-godmother," says Candy.

Erin grabs a foil-wrapped burrito marked "Beans, Rice, and Cheese," and a bottle of water, drops them both into Candy's basket. Together, they saunter up to the register. Candy tosses a handful of crumpled bills in front of the slackjawed kid standing behind the counter. "Smokes, too, red pack. And don't you dare forget matches."

Erin claims a plastic table in the front of the convenience store while Candy microwaves their burritos. Candy soon joins her, eats her burrito hungrily, but Erin only picks at hers, unimpressed by low-quality road food. Erin uncaps and takes a swig of her water, pouring it into her upturned mouth. The water is cold and clean. Erin lets a bit run down her face, onto her dusty black T-shirt.

"Oh, no," says Candy. "Looks like you made a clean spot. You should clean up before we go any further." Candy gathers up their trash, drops it into a red and yellow can, heads back into the store. Erin follows.

Candy plants her palms on the counter, leaning forward toward the clerk. The kid's eyes are magnetically drawn to her cleavage. "Quick, or I'll have to punish you. You got coin-op showers?" Candy asks him, purring. The kid looks like he might explode. "We're a couple of dirty girls. We need to get clean." He nods yes, points toward the restrooms at the back of the store. Candy reaches back and takes Erin's hand, leads her in the indicated direction. "You're a mess, Erin," says Candy as they enter the ladies room. "Look, I've got some fresh clothes in the trunk. They'll fit you. Let's get you cleaned up and presentable before we hit the City." She digs in her purse, pulls out a handful of quarters, and hands them to Erin.

"Where are we?" asks Erin.

"Santa Nella. About an hour, hour and a half away from party central. Plenty of time to get into party mode. You're coming, right?"

XXX

By the time Erin's dollar-and-a-quarter clean-up ends, Candy has managed to run their bag of provisions out to the car and return with a choice of ensembles—skirts, tops, dresses, a bag of assorted undergarments, stockings still wrapped in cardstock and cellophane, spike-heeled shoes.

"I keep all kinds of extra wardrobe in the trunk," says Candy. "Never know when you might need something. All brand new, too," she says, inspecting a dark blue stretch velvet minidress. "Nobody's spooged on 'em or anything." She scratches at a spot on the mini, drops it into the trashcan near the restroom's door.

44

Erin shimmies into a red dress, body-hugging, but still the most modest, and a pair of black fishnets. She wears her own underwear, her own dusty boots. She pulls on her leather jacket in order to cover her bra-straps and nearly bare shoulders, attends to her face with lipstick and an eye pencil produced from Candy's bag of supplies.

Erin follows Candy back out to the limo, feeling like a little girl costumed as a stripper, but noticing the way in which the kid at the counter is now watching her. It's the same sort of gaze with which he'd previously regarded Candy. It gives her a thrill, but Erin's not sure it's the sort of thrill she enjoys. As the limo hits the freeway, Candy prepares another pair of drinks. While Erin sips hers, Candy removes a pair of cigarettes from the pack, places them both between her lips, lights them, and hands one to Erin.

XXX

"What's it like," whispers Erin. "Doing it?"

"You should know," answers Candy.

Erin looks confused. "Not fucking," she says after a moment. "I mean movies."

"'S fun. Obvious you're thinking of a career change. Aren't you."

"What are you implying by 'obvious?'" says Erin.

Candy chuckles. "You're not answering my question," she says, scolding with her index finger.

"Sometimes, I guess," replies Erin, glancing down at the floor and then out the window before turning back to Candy. "I mean I don't even watch the stuff. I've seen some, sure, here and there—boyfriends, parties, hotels. I guess I could, if I had to, but..."

Candy reaches up, touches Erin's cheek, runs a finger along to her chin. "You've got a good face. Memorable. That's important. You'd think it's all about the body, all about dressing the flesh up like a sexy nun, an innocent cheerleader, a Martian go-go dancer. But it ain't. It's all about the face."

"What do you mean?"

"Guys remember faces, not bodies. Girls know our bodies are all different, but to a guy, tits are tits. But nine times out of ten, guys are the ones who buy porn, not chicks, and they want something to fixate on. We're all about the male gaze. Mostly pretty's actually better than model pretty. A well-placed freckle," Candy retrieves her finger, points to her own mouth. "A snaggletooth. They love that shit."

"Anyway—" says Erin, uncomfortably.

"Erin," interrupts Candy. "You're more than just plain hot, you've got tattoos, and I'm guessing a piercing or two. Plus, you've got attitude. Add those to that pretty face, you'd be a hit. A cover girl, for sure." Candy sets her hand on Erin's shoulder. "Seriously."

Erin leans back, breaking contact with Candy's hand. She pulls her knees up to her chin, her feet resting on the seat, and wraps her arms around them. "It's not really my thing. No offense. I like the way guys look at me, and I sometimes think, yeah, I could use this to get what I want, but I don't. I couldn't. I've got too many issues." Erin glances down again. "Besides," she says, looking back up at Candy. "What would my mom think?"

"Mine's cool with it. We even write letters and shit."

"No offense, Candy," says Erin. "It's just not my scene."

"That's cool," says Candy. "But think about this: we're alike, Erin. More than you realize. We're both entertainers. You sing your heart out, convince your audience that you're feeling all the agony, the ecstasy encoded in the lyrics. I scream 'fuck me, Daddy,' and do exactly the same thing. We're both just helping people fulfill their dreams, their fantasies."

"I guess," says Erin, glancing into her glass. She takes a piece of ice into her mouth and chews it.

"Shit, I'm not just any porn star, I own my own company. It's like Marx said, unless workers seize the means of production—and it doesn't matter if they're making widgets for midgets or music or porn—they're never gonna get anywhere. I pick my co-stars, hire my crew, cut my own tapes, and handle my own distribution."

"Marx, right," says Erin, casting a cockeyed glare at her empty glass.

"The guy with the moustache and the glasses?"

"Nah, the one with the wig and the horn. Gimme that glass, you need a refill."

XXX

They drink, they talk, and eventually, the limo hits the streets of San Francisco, arriving just as myriad streetlights are beginning to stutter on. "Are you ready to hit the best party you'll ever see?" asks Candy.

"I shouldn't," says Erin, cautiously. "That is, I ought to call my friend, figure out where to meet him, where he lives. I don't want to be ungrateful, but I really should call him."

"Okay," replies Candy. "Suit yourself. Your loss. I still think you should come with me. There are a couple of people you gotta meet. They'll like you, they like girls with tattoos. Hell, Paulie Gray's even gonna be there."

"Wait, Paulie? Paulie Gray?"

"Yeah," says Candy. "He's supposed to be playing an acoustic set, stuff for their upcoming album. Why, you know him?"

"Yeah," says Erin. "He's my friend. The one I was going to call."

"No shit? You know Paulie Gray? Why didn't you say so earlier?" She holds up her right hand, index and middle finger pressed closely together. "Me and Paulie, we're like that. Tight. Small world, eh? We're gonna have a good time."

TRACK 08
THE GREEN-EYED BEAST CALLED LOVE

On Thursday night, we head up to Orange County, to a club called the *Mise en Scène*, to catch a solo show by an old friend of Terrri named Victor E. He's one of those experimental guys, paunchy in jeans and a Destined to Fail T-shirt. Black, of course. His long hair is thinning, losing the battle with his bald spot, like Friar fucking Tuck.

Victor has a technician's approach to music theory, a mad scientist murmuring over guitar pedals instead of test tubes. For nearly an hour, he tortures an instrument that looks like a cross between a Gibson SG and a ShopVac, persuading from it an anguished array of howls, shrieks, and groans.

A few minutes after he abandons the whimpering instrument, stalking offstage in cacophonic abandon, the house DJ cuts the sound, throwing on some generic beatbox twelve-inch dance record, a panacea for the soon-gyrating crowd. Terrri leads us toward the back of the club, through a pair of leather-padded doors marked private, where Victor is standing beside a corner booth. "Glad you made it," he says. "Damn it's good to see you, Ter."

We press around the tiny table in the nightclub's offset private lounge. Victor scoots in, takes the middle, Terrri slides across the red vinyl, right up next to him, throwing her right arm around his shoulders and embracing him, hard. He grins, a gawkish, yellowed smile. I push in next to Terrri, sitting on the outside, press my hand against her knee, giving it a slight squeeze. She reaches down with her left hand, taps the back of mine twice, gives it a light scratch with her painted fingernails, wraps her fingers around mine and squeezes tight. Across from me, guarding the other end of the upholstered horseshoe, Johnny Rainbow, on the inside next to Victor, compulsively taps his pack of Lucky Strikes against the table's faux-marble surface. Maxxy Blue, gingerly seated on the cushion's edge, adjusts his makeup in a tiger-striped light-up compact. "Fuckin'-A, Vic," purrs Terrri. "What do you call that thing?"

Victor grins wider, brushes his meaty right hand through his stringy blonde hair. His gray eyes sparkle with pride. "I'm calling it an Agit-Aur. Half pure agitation, half beat-up guitar. I cobbled it together from the remains of the Adrenelator, took me weeks to figure out how to make it squawk like that. You dig it?"

"Fucking sublime," says Terrri.

Across the table, Johnny Rainbow nods in agreement while lighting his cigarette, packed to the point that its leading half inch is but a hollow paper tube. "Impressive," he says. "You rocked it."

"It was crunchy, meaty-good," says Maxxy, glancing back over his shoulder before turning back to his compact.

Victor throws his head back and laughs. "Yeah, good shit," I start to say, trailing off when I realize that the conversation's moved on without me.

Victor has turned, his left hand rests next to Terrri's cheek, touching close. "Christ," he says. "It's been too fucking long."

Terrri bats her eyelashes, mock-demurely, overstated and dramatic, then sighs, genuine. "Yeah," she says. "It's good to see you, too."

A waitress presses through the door, and for a moment a burst from the club's electro-pop fill music intrudes upon our scene. Maxxy clicks his compact shut, and announces, "I'm going to go out there and dance, dance, dance." He stands up, makes an unnecessary show of smoothing out his leather miniskirt, and disappears through the door back into the noisy club. The waitress, attractive from across the room but worn and weather-beaten beneath her caked-on makeup, approaches our table and takes our order: a pitcher of Newcastle, a tray of assorted appetizers, and a bottle of Buckler for Victor. Once she, too, has vanished back into the world of noise, Victor leans back, looks at Terrri, and says, "So, what brings you up the river to Hell-A, anyway?"

Terrri drums her fingernails against the tabletop. "What, Colonel Kurtz," she says. "Can't I just make a social call? Check up on an old friend?"

"We both know you're not like that," says Victor. "You're only here because you want something."

Terrri sighs, glances down at the table, then over at Johnny Rainbow. Johnny holds out the pack of cigarettes, which Terrri takes. She plucks one from the pack, hands the pack back to Johnny, places the cigarette between her lips. I start to reach for my lighter, but Victor is quicker, producing a book of paper matches, striking one, and lighting Terrri's cigarette. Johnny tucks the pack back into his shirt pocket. "Okay," she says. "To business it is."

Terrri takes a long drag from her cigarette, exhales a plume of smoke into the air, holds it out to me without looking over. I take it. "Vic," she says. "We're about three-quarters of the way into recording the new record out at Southern Cross. Johnny's written cello parts on two songs. Billy Markus from the label brought in some skeezy little chick that he's probably fucking to play 'em, but she was terrible, no tone at all, big waste of time and money. We could overdub them with synth, but I was hoping to talk you into coming down and re-tracking the parts. We're already over budget, so it'll only be scale, but you'll get full credit in the liner notes." She touches his shoulder gently with her right hand. "Please, for me?"

Victor crosses his arms in front of his chest, pushing his already pronounced biceps forward, then bites his lower lip as if thinking. "Who's running the boards?" he asks.

"Denny Lane," she answers.

"He's good," volunteers Johnny. I nod, even though I think the guy's an unbearable asshole.

"Yeah," says Victor. "I know him. He's got a rep, but I don't have any problems with the guy."

The waitress presses back through the noisy door, bearing tray and pitcher. She sets down the pitcher, platter of miscellaneous appetizers, five plates, four glasses, stack of napkins, and Victor's Buckler. "Need anything else, hon?" she asks, of nobody in particular.

"No, thanks, we're good," says Johnny. He picks up a steaming deep-fried cheese stick, swirls it about in something vaguely resembling ranch dressing, then chomps into it. Johnny exhales sharply. "Fuck, that's hot!" he exclaims, grabbing a glass, half-filling it from the pitcher, and quickly tossing it back. Terrri looks up at the waitress and smiles, rolls her eyes, turns her attention back to Victor.

"Suit yourselves," says the waitress, before vanishing through the door. I fill a glass for myself, one for Terrri, and top up Johnny's. Johnny quickly picks his up, drinking to soothe his scorched tongue.

Terrri touches Victor's shoulder again. "So, you'll do it?" she asks.

"When would you want me?" he responds, taking a swig from his bottle.

"Next week?"

"Too soon," replies Victor. "Caff's got doctor's appointments like every single day. I could probably squeeze in a day or two week after, get the nurse to watch her. I'd need to check."

Terrri picks up her beer and takes a swig, then sets the glass down, a clear lipstick print on the rim. "Shit," she says, looking down at the table. "I'm sorry. I'm just so caught up in my own shit right now. I really should have asked how she's doing earlier."

Victor reaches out with his left hand, takes Terrri's chin in it, forcing eye contact. The silver ring on his finger glints in spite of the lounge's low light. "She's good," he says, letting go. "At least as good as can be expected. The new meds seem to be helping, taking the edge off her pain. Some days are good, some are bad."

Victor brushes the back of his hand against the corner of his right eye. "You know, she got me through my worst, got me clean, got me my life, my music back." He takes another swig of the Buckler. "It's the least I can do, 'for better or worse,' you know."

Johnny gets up from the table. "I need to hit the head," he announces before briskly crossing the lounge and exiting through the door.

Terrri reaches back, takes my hand in hers, squeezes it tight. "She loves you, Vic," she says. "You know she does."

"Yeah, I know," he says, brushing his hand against his eyes again. "It's just rough. You knew her, so adventurous, so alive. Now it wears her out just moving from the bed to the couch." He drives his fist into the tabletop. "Christ, they can't even figure out what's wrong with her."

Terrri lets go of my hand, reaches forward, touches Victor's shoulder. "She loves you, Vic," she repeats. "You know she does." I run my hand up Terrri's back to her neck, feeling her long hair brush my hand as I ascend.

When I touch her neck, she looks back, shooting me a gelicidal glance, so I let go, reach for my glass, and drain it. "I'm going to go find Johnny and Maxxy," I announce, then head out, alone, into the noise and commotion of the club.

XXX

We drive almost all the way back to Garageland without talking, without radio, Johnny Rainbow behind the wheel of the van, Terrri staring out the passenger window, and me squeezed in between them. Behind us, Maxxy Blue sleeps, stretched out on the back seat, occasionally interrupting the silence with his murmuring and snores. Finally, Terrri speaks. "Christ, that was depressing," she says.

"Yeah," agrees Johnny. "But at least he's going to do it."

"So it was worth the trip," I volunteer.

"I guess," says Terrri. She takes my hand in hers, holds it tight. "I'd just hate to be in his spot." She frowns, looks down, then looks up again, smiling. "Hope I die before I get old," she says. Around us, the lights of the freeway fall past, disappear into the distance, alone and uncaring.

TRACK 09
PRINCIPALITIES AND THRONES

As he rotates a wineglass in his hand, Paulie Gray contemplates the value of the human soul. He notes the deep and sanguine swirl of the liquid, the viscous way it clings to the crystal sides. One soul, human. Well-used, slightly tarnished. He inventories, sips at his wine. Paulie rolls the mouthful across his tongue, notes the flavors of fruit, of earth, of gunpowder. He closes his eyes.

"There's no sacrifice too great," he says aloud. "For a chance at immortality." Paulie opens his eyes. "Bogart said that in a movie, once."

Mister Sturm is still there, sitting across the suite's coffee table from Paulie, still grinning carnivorously. Paulie had hoped the dark-suited man, as well as his doppelganger companion, Mister Drang, would have disappeared when his eyes reopened. No such luck. Sturm still stares and grins. Drang still paces. Paulie picks up his glass, drains it, sets the empty wineglass back on the cluttered table. Sturm speaks. "Bogart, yes. I believe we own the rights to several of his films. Classics, all. We could send you copies. Would you like a bit more wine, Mister Gray, sir?"

"Oh, yes," says Mister Drang. "Do have more, have more." He rubs his hands together. "It's best that you be in a receptive frame of mind before we talk business."

Paulie frowns at the mention of business, then leans back in his chair. "Sure," he says. "I could do with a refill."

Mister Drang crosses the room, picks up the bottle from the far side of the table, refills Paulie's glass. He sets the bottle down, and pulls a small silver case from the breast pocket of his suit jacket, which he snicks open.

"Cigarette?" he offers. "Or perhaps something stronger?"

"No, no," replies Paulie, waving Drang and his cigarettes away. He picks up his glass, examines it as he swirls it again. "Nothing." Paulie stares into the dark fluid as if it were a scrying ball. For a moment he looks as if he is about to divine the future, then he takes a sip. He swallows. "This really is quite lovely," says Paulie Gray.

"The vintage?" asks Drang, snapping his cigarette case closed and replacing it in his pocket. "Oh, yes. We can have it sent to you by the case. It's one of our more popular perks. Imported, you know."

"Ah," says Paulie. He takes another drink, again closes his eyes, swishes the liquid around in his mouth. Even with his eyes closed, Paulie feels as if Sturm's eyes are capable of boring a pathway straight through to his soul. "Imported," repeats Paulie.

"Of course," says Drang. "The finer things in life often are." Paulie reopens his eyes. Sturm is still staring, wolfish.

"Look," says Paulie. "I said it before. I need to talk to Marco before I sign anything."

"Of course," replies Drang. "But rest assured, Zion-I Records is certain to realize that forging an association between you and our organization would be to everyone's financial benefit."

"Trust us on this," hisses Mister Sturm, rubbing his hands. "Only our organization has the resources to adequately take you and The Paulie Gray Band to the next level. It's in your best interest, the band's best interest, Marco's best interest." He picks up his clipboard of papers from the table, thrusting them toward Paulie. "You might as well sign. That way, everybody wins."

Paulie runs his hand across his dreadlocked hair, pushing it back from his eyes. He takes another sip of wine. "Not until I have a chance to talk with Marco. Marco and I have a history. You guys, on the other hand," Paulie says, pointing first at Sturm, then at Drang, using the index finger of the hand that holds his glass. "I'm still figuring out whether I trust you."

XXX

Two girls, one blonde, one dark-haired, are stepping off the elevator as Paulie shows Sturm and Drang into the hallway. "I really hope we can do business together, Mister Gray," says Drang, but Paulie's attention has been drawn away, captured by the girls. The ever-welcome Candy Snowdrop, thinks Paulie, and one of her little friends. This should be fun.

"Yeah, yeah," responds Paulie, dismissively, ushering the two men toward the elevator. "Hey Candy," he says, turning to her and touching the small of her back. "Delivery?"

She holds up the canvas bag she's carried in from the limo and shakes it. "Yep! Candy delivery." She leans forward, gives him a peck on the cheek.

He smiles, turns his attention to the other girl, navigating his eyes upward from her boots to her shapely legs to her hip-clutching short skirt. She's carrying a black, zip-up guitar case. "Who's your..." He starts to say "friend," but as he arrives on Erin's face, stretches out the "f," shifting instead to say, "f-f-fuck, Erin Locke. No shit. Fuck, it's good to see you." He throws his arms around her leather-jacketed form, drawing her into a bear hug. "Fuck," he repeats, nodding his head. "It's good to see you."

"Hi Paulie," says Erin, squeezed breathless. "Good to see you too."

"Touching, touching," comments Candy, crossing her arms and tapping one foot dramatically. She reaches out, grasps Paulie's bicep with one hand, then points the other's index finger at his chest, right above his heart. "But see here. We're two dangerous broads. We're on the lam and looking for action. Where's the party?"

"Let's hit the room and check out that delivery," says Paulie, pointing at her satchel then glancing at his watchless wrist. "It's early yet. We've got a couple of hours to kill. Come on." He slides an arm around Erin's waist, smiling at her. "Catch me up," he says, sliding the other arm around Candy's waist. "And after that I'll show you two how to party."

XXX

It takes Paulie several tries to force his key into the lock, though he laughs off his clumsiness as the unfortunate result of too much drink, too much fun, too much partying. Candy and Erin, in similar straits, lean against one another, passing a bottle of bourbon back and forth between fits of laughter. Paulie turns the key, opens the door, and proceeds to drop his key to the floor as he removes it from the lock. Candy laughs hard enough that she falls back into a wall, nearly upsetting a glass-topped table and lamp before sliding to the floor, giggling the entire time. She looks up from where she sits, leaning against the gold wallpaper. "I fall down," she calls to Erin and Paulie. "Go boom." She points. "Oh, hey. You dropped your key."

Erin holds out her hands. "Come on, Miss Tipsy. Let's get you up." Candy clasps Erin's wrists in her hands, but instead of being pulled up, she pulls Erin down to the floor.

"Much better," says Candy, looking down at Erin. "You were awfully far away up there."

Erin sits up, scoots next to Candy by the wall. She cups her hands above her eyes, looking up at Paulie. "I see what you mean," she says. "How do you propose we bring him down here?"

Candy strokes her chin. "Good question," she replies. "We could trip him."

"Kick him?" asks Erin, taking the bottle from Candy, wiping the neck against the sleeve of her leather jacket, taking a long swig. "Oh, I know. Unplug that lamp. We'll tie him up."

Candy takes back the bottle, swigs without wiping. "Girl, I like the way you think." She reaches up and sets the empty bottle on the table.

Paulie crosses his arms in front of his chest, swaying slightly as he does so. "You two are drunk, drunk as a couple of fucking drunks," he says. He uncrosses his arms, waves a finger at them, mock-scolding them. "Now get in the room before somebody calls security. It's, like, three in the fucking morning." He gestures toward the open door and the blackness beyond.

Candy salutes. "Yeth thir," she lisps. She stretches her arms, reaching skyward, maneuvers herself into a kneeling position. "Aye, aye, captain," says Candy, proceeding to crawl across the carpeted hallway on hands and knees and through the doorway of the hotel room.

Erin looks up at Paulie with a shrug. "Why the fuck not?" she asks nobody in particular, follows Candy into the room, crawling as well. As she passes Paulie, she looks up, meows, shakes her ass, laughs as she crosses the threshold.

XXX

Stepping into the room, Paulie stoops and pockets his key, closes the door, and slides the chain into place. He pauses, contemplating the long night ahead, reopens the door the length of the chain. Reaching out, he hangs the "do not disturb" sign on the knob, before finally closing and bolting the door. His task completed, Paulie turns to find that the girls have already claimed their own places in the suite.

Erin lounges on the couch as Candy rifles through the suite's minibar. She holds a tiny bottle of vodka aloft, illuminated by the cold white light of the refrigerator. "Hey Paulie," she shouts. "You got anything bigger than kid-sized?"

Paulie pulls his key from his pocket and drops it onto the table next to the television. "Back in the bedroom," he says, pulling his still-buttoned shirt over his head and mopping his brow with it. "There should be a bottle or two in there. Those label stiffs brought me a bunch of stuff." He tosses the shirt onto the table, concealing his key.

Candy tosses the vodka back into the minibar fridge, then strolls toward the bedroom door. "Say," suggests Paulie. "You mind breaking out a bit of that delivery, rolling one?"

"You got it, babe," says Candy, disappearing into the bedroom. "I'm not done having fun yet. Oh, hey, you got any ice?" she calls from within.

"Ice, yeah," says Paulie. "Back in a flash." He turns back toward the door, remembers the ice bucket, stops, retraces his steps, grabs the bucket, unlocks, unchains the door, and steps out into the hall.

XXX

Erin stretches out on the couch, using her leather jacket as a pillow. She yawns, begins to unlace her boots. Candy returns carrying a pair of plastic-wrap-covered glasses and a bottle of Jack Daniel's. Her canvas satchel is tucked under one arm. "Where's Paulie?" she asks.

"Ice," says Erin. "Remember?" She drops one boot to the floor with a thump and starts working at the laces of the other one, proceeding to make a knotted mess of the bow. Candy interrupts her, pressing a glass into her hand, setting the other glass and her satchel on an end table. Erin fusses with the plastic wrap, and by the time she's managed to remove it, Candy is ready to pour. Three fingers of whiskey for Erin, three fingers for Candy.

Erin takes a sip and leans back on the couch, lifting her mismatched feet into the air. She twists the one with the boot at the ankle, back and forth, back and forth. She takes another drink. "Looks like I forgot something," she laughs.

"Gimme that," says Candy, flopping down onto the couch next to Erin and grabbing her feet. She tugs at Erin's laces, resorts to fingernails and, within a few moments, manages to loosen the mess. She wrests the boot from Erin's foot and tosses it to the ground with a thud. "See, teamwork gets it done." Candy takes one of Erin's feet in hand, rubbing it. Her hands are soft, smooth, and, Erin realizes, surprisingly strong.

"Mmmm... Hey... Oh. That's the spot," mumbles Erin, closing her eyes. "Obviously you've done this before."

Candy laughs. "Honey, I've done just about everything at least once before. When I found stuff I liked, I did it twice."

"Got it," says Erin, opening her eyes. "Say, you and Paulie, are you, like..."

"Like what?" laughs Candy. "A couple? An item? Involved? Fucking?"

"Well, yeah," says Erin, sitting up. "I mean I'm just trying to figure out if I need to stay out of the way, sleep on the couch or something, you know."

"Don't sweat it," says Candy. "If anybody's going to have to stay out of the way, it's going to be Paulie." She grasps Erin's foot, then slides her hand upward, caressing Erin's ankle, her calf, the back of her knee.

"Ummm..." says Erin, closing her eyes again. "About that..."

XXX

Ice bucket in hand, Paulie starts down the hallway toward the floor's ice machine. But when he arrives, he finds an "out of order" sign hanging on the metal door. "Aw, shit," says Paulie, thumping his fist against the side of the machine.

Paulie wanders back toward the room, stands at the door for a moment listening to the laughter within, shrugs, crosses to the elevator. He stabs the down button with his index finger, twirling the empty ice bucket in his other hand. As he waits for the elevator car to arrive, he drums on the bottom of the bucket with his fingers, tapping out a simple syncopated rhythm. The car arrives and the door slides open. Empty. Paulie rides down to the next floor, disembarks, and heads for the ice machine. There, he fills his bucket, then wanders back to the elevator and presses the up button.

This time, when the door slides open, the car isn't empty. Instead, a pair of blonde women in their mid-forties tumble out, drunk. "Hey, handsome," says one, pointing at Paulie with an index finger. "You looking for a party?"

"Are you lost?" asks the other. She laughs at her own joke, tipping her head back to reveal a number of filled teeth.

Paulie smiles politely, noticing their worn business wear, their thickly made-up faces. "Just picking up a little bit of ice," he says, indicating his bucket.

One of the women steps forward, tottering a bit on her high heels, and presses her palm against Paulie's bare chest. "You have anywhere in particular you were planning to stick it?" she asks, pointing at the ice bucket. She snatches a piece of ice and pops it into her mouth, crunching it between her teeth.

The other woman grasps Paulie's shoulder with both hands, leaning forward to whisper into Paulie's ear. Her breath is hot, desperate. "Chewing ice is a sure sign of sexual frustration."

"Is it?" responds Paulie. The elevator door begins to slide shut, so Paulie extends a foot to interrupt its closure. He feigns a yawn. "It's late. I should get back up to my room."

The woman with the ice cube places her hand against Paulie's chest again, migrates it downward along Paulie's torso, tracing a finger down his abs, past his belt buckle. "Is anything else pierced?" she asks, eyeing his ringed nipples. She rubs her hand against the crotch of his leather pants. Paulie feels his cock begin to stiffen, even though the women remind him of stuffed sausages.

"What do you say, you wanna make a sandwich?" whispers the other woman into his ear, licking his earlobe for punctuation. "You can be the meat."

"Um, look, ladies," says Paulie. "I'm flattered, really, but I've got to go." He pushes past them into the elevator, then jabs "door close" and his floor number with index and pinky. As the door slides shut, a shoe flies through, carried on the epithets shouted by the two women. "Fucking faggot! God damned queer!" Paulie leans against the side of the ascending car, chuckling.

XXX

Paulie digs through his pockets when he arrives back at the room, realizing that he's left his key inside. He listens at the door, hears music. He knocks. The music stops. "Leave us alone," shouts Candy's voice. "We're fucking." Erin's laughter follows.

"Shit," says Paulie, dropping to the floor and sitting. "Shit," he repeats.

The door swings open, restrained by its security chain. Candy peeks out, looks down at Paulie. "Quick, what's the password?" she asks. The scent of high-quality marijuana leaks through the cracked-open door.

Paulie holds aloft the ice bucket. "Room service?" he offers.

"Hang on," says Candy, closing the door. Half a minute passes. The door reopens. This time, Erin stands looking past the chain. "What's the password?" she asks.

"Jesus H. tap-dancing Christ, you crazy, drunk-assed bitches," suggests Paulie. "Let me the fuck in."

Erin closes the door, and Paulie listens to the slide of the chain before she reopens it. "Good guess," she says. "We just changed it."

XXX

On the couch, Candy laughs. She holds a blazing joint between two fingers. The television is on, showing *Jesus Christ Superstar* with the volume turned all the way down. Onscreen, Ted Neeley crosses his eyes earnestly. Erin runs back to the couch, jumps on next to Candy, who holds the joint up to Erin's lips. Erin takes a hit. Paulie closes and chains the door behind him, crosses the room, and leans against the back of the couch, hands behind each girl's shoulders. "Why's the volume off?"

Erin exhales an expansive blue cloud of smoke, coughs a little, then says, "'Cause we were doing the singin'."

"Who's singing who?" asks Paulie. Candy hands him the joint. He inhales with a slight whistle.

Candy points at Erin, "She's Jesus," she says. "I'm Judas." She points to herself. "And we been trading off everybody else."

"Oh, yeah?" Paulie moves to hand the joint to Erin, but she just stares at the screen. He offers it back to Candy, but she's watching the television as well. Paulie takes another hit.

Suddenly, Erin turns, grabbing Paulie's arm. "Oh, hey! Herod's coming up. You sing Herod."

Candy turns as well. "Yeah, do Herod."

"Only if I get to do Pilate, too," smirks Paulie.

"Deal," says Erin, pointing at the screen. "Oh, go. You're on."

They smoke, and drink, and sing, making up whatever words they don't remember, until the hippies board their bus and drive away, leaving Jesus behind, hanging on his cross. "Fuckers," says Candy. "I can't believe they just leave him in the desert and shit."

"It's a metaphor," says Paulie, now sitting between the two girls on the couch. They both lean against him, Erin tracing patterns with her fingernail on his chest. "Or a symbol or something. He doesn't ride in with them, he just shows up all of a sudden when they're dancing around." Paulie leans forward, displacing Erin. He picks up the bottle of Jack Daniel's from the table, takes a swig, wipes his mouth, and sets the bottle back down again. He leans back, stretches his arm out onto Erin's shoulders, and pulls her toward him. "That felt good," he says. "In any case, Candy," he turns his head toward her as Erin resumes her tracing. "It's only a movie."

"Yeah," says Erin. "But we rocked it."

"You were better than Neeley," says Paulie, looking down at Erin's slightly out-of-focus face where she leans against his shoulder. "But you're no Ian Gillian."

Candy laughs. "Fuck you," says Erin, sweetly. She loops a pinky finger through the ring piercing Paulie's nipple and gives it a tug for emphasis. She looks up at him. "I'll bet you wish I was Ian Gillian." She pokes him in the ribs. "Fag," she says, taunting.

"I'll show you fag," he says, squeezing her tighter with his arm around her shoulders. He kisses the top of her head. The end credits of *Jesus Christ Superstar* give way to *Barbarella*. "Ooh," says Paulie. "Somebody turn up the volume."

Candy gets up, walks over to the TV, and turns it up. She yawns, stretching, the blue light of the television transforming her into an hourglass silhouette. She sashays back to the couch, flops down opposite Erin, resting her head against Paulie's other shoulder. The three of them sit, staring at the TV. By the time Jane Fonda has completed her zero-G striptease, Paulie, Erin, and Candy have drifted off to sleep.

Erin awakens to the sound of Durand Durand's Barbarella-imprisoning organ. She focuses on the screen, chuckles lightly at Fonda's flustered faux-orgasmic face, then looks up at Paulie's face. His eyes are closed. His lips quiver slightly as he exhales. She inhales the familiar scent of his bare skin as her eyes trace their way down his profile, noting the way in which the light of the television lends a halo to each tiny hair.

Erin's eyes continue their downward path, down his neck, pausing at Paulie's Adam's apple, watching as he swallows. She moves down past his collarbone, to the heaving muscular landscape of his chest. She imagines that she can feel his heart beating through the layers of skin and bone and sinew. Erin's gaze descends further, trickling down Paulie's ribs, his abdomen. She kisses his shoulder, plays at his chest with her fingertips. The drink, the smoke, the proximity, realizes Erin, has her excited, aroused. She shifts her legs, crossing them, kisses Paulie's shoulder again.

Erin directs her eyes further down Paulie's body, concentrating upon the well of his navel. She considers dipping her tongue into it, arousing him, awakening him with a navel assault. She chuckles at her own joke, then inches her way further down. Erin gasps, realizing that Paulie's belt is undone, his leather pants unbuttoned. Candy's hand, red-nailed, a hand Erin knows is as strong as it is soft, caresses the erect shaft of Paulie's cock. The tip of it glistens in the television light.

Erin brings her eyes back up Paulie's prone body, feeling him shudder against her face as she climbs the surface of his skin. Across his chest, she meets eyes with Candy. "Hey you," says Candy. She lightly kisses the surface of Paulie's skin. "You wanna fuck him?"

"Yeah," says Erin, biting her lower lip. Candy smiles.

"You wanna kiss me? I can keep a secret."

"Sure," says Erin. "Why not?"

Candy moistens her lips with the tip of her tongue. "Wake up, sleepyhead," she says, tightening her grip on Paulie's cock. "I'm sure you don't want to miss this."

Paulie opens his eyes to see Erin and Candy, profiles backlit by the television screen, leaning in across his chest, mouths intertwined, tongues tied. The sensation of Candy's grip along the shaft of his cock intensifies as Erin's hand joins it, stroking its base with string-calloused fingertips. The girls' mouths separate, a gleaming strand of spittle connecting them for an instant, then breaking. At that moment, Paulie explodes, closing his eyes and ejaculating onto himself.

"Aw, yeah," says Candy, laughing. "That's what I'm talking about." She dips a finger into the come pooled in Paulie's navel, uses it to trace letters on his chest. *Candy and Erin were here*, she writes.

"Was that good?" asks Erin, nuzzling up to Paulie's ear.

"Oh, yeah," he answers.

"Better question," says Candy. "Are you going to carry us off to the bedroom and fuck us now, or are you spent?" She licks her finger clean.

Paulie looks down at his wilting erection, the mess covering his torso. He looks at Candy, at Erin. Erin arches an eyebrow. "Well?" she says. "Are you man enough for the task, or are Candy and I going to have to work this out for ourselves?"

Paulie stands up, holds out his hands. Candy takes one; Erin, the other. "Oh, I think I can manage," he says, pulling them up. "Come on."

XXX

By the time the afternoon sun starts peeking through the corners of the bedroom's blackout curtains, Candy has disappeared, heading off to her own adventures, leaving behind pleasant memories and the unspoken promise of future encounters. Erin and Paulie lie naked, exposed, like fine rock and roll. An atoll of sheets is scattered around them, framing them in tableau, entwined upon the ocean-wide mattress. "Hey Paulie," says Erin, resting her head against his bare chest. Her eyes are closed, and she absentmindedly traces tiny circles around his nipple, slips her pinky through the ring that pierces it. "What now? I mean, what happens next? With us, I mean."

"I guess I take you to meet the band," he says, scratching his leg. "The record's in the can, so it's really just a question of learning the songs. Marco's scheduling the tour dates, so all you've really got to worry about is getting up to speed. You've got a couple of weeks for that."

"Just understand," says Erin. "I'm not some one-night fuck-toy, some fucking chick bassist. I'm not content to be a rock star's girlfriend. I'm not interested in just being the broad in the publicity photo. If I'm in, I'm in all the way, or not at all. I'll play bass for you, sure, but I'm doing vocals too. My songs." She sits up, holding her hand against her chest for emphasis. "My songs."

"Yeah, sure," says Paulie, leaning across the bed and picking up his guitar. "We can make that work. Here, get your bass, try this one," he says. "It's in A minor. It's called 'Principalities and Thrones.' Think *Faust*, but from Mephistopheles' point of view."

"Mephistopheles?" asks Erin.

"The Devil. You do know *Faust*, right?"

"Krautrock band?" she answers, rising and retrieving her bass from the other room. "Early 70s. Contemporaries of Kraftwerk. Electronics and synthesizers, spooky shit, right?"

"Um, no. *Faust* is a play. It's about a guy who sells his soul to the devil."

"Why?" Erin unzips her case, removes her bass, sits opposite Paulie on the bed, cross-legged with the bass in her lap. "Gimme an E."

"Why what?" asks Paulie. He plucks the E string on his guitar. She turns a knob on the head of her bass, tunes to match his tone.

"Why's he sell his soul?" asks Erin. "What for? What's in it for Faust?"

"The usual," answers Paulie, scratching his head. "Money, power, happiness..."

"Sex?" she suggests.

"Yeah, there's a girl. Her name's Gretchen. But Faust kind of fucks that up. Repeatedly. It's a long play."

"There's a trial, right?" asks Erin, continuing to tune her bass.

"Ummm... you're thinking of *The Devil and Daniel Webster*."

"Nope," she shakes her head. "I'm thinking of *The Devil and Daniel Mouse*. I always wanted to be Funky Jan when I grew up. I guess maybe I pulled it off."

"You did, didn't you?" asks Paulie. "Except for the part about her being a mouse, y'know?" He strums a series of power chords. "You're anything but a mouse. Here, follow along. Like I said, A minor."

"A minor," repeats Erin. "And after this, I'm going to show you how to play 'A Killing.'"

"You've got it," says Paulie. "Then maybe I'll call room service. I'm starving. Two, three, four..."

XXX

Mister Sturm sits across the coffee table from Erin and Paulie, his long, canine face twisted, as usual, into a rictus approximation of a grin. Behind him, Mister Drang paces back and forth, explaining the terms of the latest draft of the contract. They wear the same suits as they did when Paulie saw them last, one week ago. "So, as you can see," says Drang, hands gesturing as he speaks. "Our latest offer provides not only for distribution and tour support while leaving creative and management decisions to you and your..." he pauses, indicating Erin with an extended hand, "...associates, but we will also purchase the assets of Zion-I Records outright, allowing Marco to stay onboard and manage your back catalogue. You will, of course, be able to continue to take your career in the musical direction you see fit. And, as the young lady requested," he grimaces, closing his eyes as if in pain, "you will retain ownership of your masters." Mister Drang opens his eyes, smiles. "Everybody wins."

"It should all be quite lucrative," hisses Sturm, sliding his crowded clipboard across the table. "Just sign at the bottom, on each of the three top sheets, and we'll take care of the rest."

Paulie picks up his wineglass from the table, rolling it in his fingers, noticing his reflection in the bloodred rippled surface of the wine.

He glances at Erin, sipping wine from her own glass. She is wearing Paulie's Bad Brains T-shirt with the pair of black jeans he bought for her a few days earlier. She meets his eyes, lowers the glass from her lips, smiling. "It's your call, Paulie," she says. "I'm not going to argue with a paycheck."

Paulie sets his glass back on the table, then picks up the clipboard, glancing down at its paragraphs of legalistic language. He runs a finger along its surface. The party of the first part. Mister Sturm holds out a silver pen. "At the bottom," he says. "Right on the line."

Paulie takes pen in hand, weighs it. It is cold, solid, and heavy. He turns it over and over between his fingertips. One soul, human, muses Paulie. Well-used, only slightly tarnished. He glances back to Erin. She smiles at him with wine-stained lips. With Mister Sturm's pen held tightly in his right hand, Paulie signs the contract.

TRACK 10
CHRISTIAN SAYS

Distant dreaming drums in the darkness. Savage, martial, ritual. Far enough to be the whispered beat beneath the ocean's sanguine roar, the gasping inhalations and exhalations of a dying world.

You sit above the mighty ocean, a tall, sheer wall separating you from crashing waves, their inward roll, breaking across shattered monoliths, a freeway cacophony. The waves' retreat is the gentle marimba of settling stones trapped in the hollows between civilizations' broken, jutting teeth. Voices call from the distance, whispers beneath the smash and collapse, crying for salvation within the flotsam. You ignore these plaintive cries.

Smoke billows, black and acrid, stinging your eyes, echoed in miniature by the cigarette tucked between your left index and middle fingers. Cities burn: skyscrapers, business parks, stave churches, nightclubs, amusement parks. Across the channel, across the sea, dragons circle, snatching survivors clinging to the peaks of drowning buildings, belching flames at lifeboats, fires that burn, continuous and sticky on the water's surface.

You wear a fast-food cardboard crown upon your head.

You reach out and down, your right hand grasping at a bottleneck beside your lonely throne. You push the cork away with your calloused thumb, watching as it flies and falls, bounding against the cliff wall as it tumbles to the sea, as it joins the debris bobbing on the surface, indistinguishable from wreckage.

You drink.

Wine, blood-red and dark flows across your lips, your savaged teeth, your bloated tongue. You taste the ocean's salt. You taste drowning souls, plummeting down your gullet, in freefall. You taste the bitterness of sacrifice, the ripened rhythms of fauns crushing grapes in sylvan glades. You feel the alcoholic warmth of conquering, of drinking down your fears, regrets, ghosts.

You glance down at the bottle in your hand. Below the neck, the shoulder, the body is a burnished skull, jaw missing, its left side covered in cracks, its orbit, its zygomatic arch shattered, as if by a headfirst Phaëton fall, or unfortunate collision with the tires of a massive truck, or both. The smoke, the fires, your eyes are reflected on the surface of the blood-black liquid visible through the glassed-in openings. You take another swig, roll the wine around in your mouth, savoring it.

"Whatever," you say, dismissively crushing your cigarette on the arm of your throne, which you realize now is made up of more human skulls. You are perched atop a pile of your fallen enemies. *How cliché.* The butt continues to smolder. You tuck the bottle between your legs, facing out to share your view, pull the pack of smokes from your jacket pocket, tap it thirteen times against the palm of your hand. You pluck another from the pack, offer it to the grim bottle. "Want one?"

Fuck you.

"Suit yourself." You replace the pack and pull the kid's lighter from your watch pocket. You click it open, roll the wheel against your leg, igniting it.

You inhale deep, drawing smoke into your lungs. A dragon passes overhead, a supersonic roar. You feel the heat as it rumbles by, a screaming youth clutched in its jaws. You shift the cigarette to your left hand, grasp the bottle by the neck and bring it to your lips, take another blood-black swig. Cain, sating himself on brother-blood. You wipe your mouth against your sleeve, take another pull, draining the bottle.

You hold the skull by the neck above your mouth, letting a final drop dribble onto your tongue, then launch it into the blackness, watch it spin with abandon as it arcs and glances back, facing you one final time before plummeting into the black abyss. You hear it shattering on the stones. You gaze downward, expecting to see the face staring back at you, but it is lost to the sea, a ghost drowned in an endless ocean.

You think of Tish, supine at your feet, clasping at your leg in supplication as you rule this gasping, dying world from your throne of bones. "Tish," you say, and you can taste her as you say her name. You reach for her, expecting to run your fingers through her long, black hair, but touch nothing, a ghost, an empty promise.

She looks up at you, hair blowing back in the everpresent wind.

Her face a skull.

Your eyes open.

XXX

The practice space is dark, the stained carpet covering the drum riser rough against your face. You sit up, holding your arms tight against your chest in an attempt to warm up. *Fucking dreams*, you say to yourself, then thrust your hand into a pocket in search of another painkiller.

You wrap your fingers around a pill, indifferent to which kind, washing it down with the two inches of warm beer left from last night. "Fucking dreams," you say aloud, tossing the empty bottle into a corner. You pick up the half-smoked roach from the floor nearby and light it with the kid's skull lighter, wrestled from the watch pocket of your jeans. You smoke it down until it burns your cracked, chapped lips, your yellow-stained fingers, crush what remains into the carpet. You stand up, stretch, listen to the crack of your back, stressed from weeks of sleeping on the floor. Your mouth tastes of sleep and beer and smoke. Your muscles ache, despite the flow of cannabinoids through your blood, the release of endorphins, dynorphin, enkephalins, into your system.

You climb into the seat of the trap and pull a pair of sticks from the scabbard, each one sixty-six grams of American Hickory, stained dark as fear and night itself. Wooden tips, none of this plastic-coated shit.

You grip the shafts, twirl them in your fingers. Precision instruments, little rituals. Drumstick daggers. A matched pair of black-handled sonic knives. Magick wands beat against a drumskin pentacle.

You slide your right foot into the metal shoe of the bass pedal and stamp out three short bursts. The sound—low and rich and strong—fills the carpet-walled space, an invocation, opened, summoning the gods of noise and chaos, of revenge.

You warm up. A quick pattern on the snare, across the toms and onto the floor tom. You work snare and bass and ride, pumping, pushing against the very fabric of time, inserting as many strokes as you can muster into the beat that is the cosmic metronome.

The spirits of a thousand dark and drumming shamans begin to ascend the spiral staircase of your spine, a continuum of devil drums, bare hands against goatskinned djembe, tabla, frenzied bodhrán. Kief-crazed tebel players, red-eyed and ecstatic, begin to chant, drawing down Pan, Bou Jeloud, the slavering goat-god of dark-dreaming night, the Father of Fear. Military tattoos sound, calling up the hungry, doglike battlefield gods of violence and depravity. Sound of drums, thunder.

You release your body to these spirits. Your feet, your hands, arms, shoulders all synchronize, inhabit the rhythm, the heartbeat, the pace. You half-close your eyes, lost on the percussive current, lolling your head back and forth on the sonic tide. You are unaware of the rivulets of sweat that stream down your face, your quickened pulse, the steam that rises from your body in the night's chill air. You are one, the drummer and the drum. The force of falling sticks, the vibration of the skin. You are the rhythm; the rhythm, you.

Your eyes begin to dance behind their shielding lids, inviting a torrent of images, projections against the cavern wall that is your mind. You think of Tish and she manifests—a touch, a moment lost replaying in your head. She, astride you, her bare skin luminescent in candlelight. She, pinioned to you, arched over you, her elegant palms pressed against your shoulders, her pale feet intertwined with yours. Her hips rock to and fro, oceanic in their rhythm, their steady ebb and flow. She gasps, shudders, buries her face in the contours of your skin, nuzzling your ear as she whispers Gnostic secrets. Her hair, scented like cedar, like lavender, plays across your face. "Oh, Christian," she murmurs, cupping your face in her hands. "I could lose myself in you."

She presses her lips to yours and begins to explore the confines, the secrets of your open mouth with her tongue. She draws your breath, your very soul into her own. Her tongue glides along, tasting, teasing, twisting around yours, enfolding and enrapturing. You feel the tip of it slide along the pearly battlements that are your teeth. It hesitates a moment, plunges deep into the septic cavern, the battered and devastated wreckage left in the wake of Robbie's pummeling assault.

She pulls away, wiping her mouth against the back of her hand. Her skin begins to wither, desiccate. Green fire rages in her sinking eyes. Her long black hair turns grey, brittle, then starts to fall away. Her lips draw back, her nose sinking into a cavity, a cartilage-tipped ruin. Her face a skull, Tish tilts her head and looks at you through empty, burning sockets. "Oh, Christian," she says. "How could you?"

And she is gone, vanished. Your hands, your feet, however, take no notice. They continue to wrack their rhythmic recitations of stick and drum and spirit. Erin Locke appears next before your entranced and fluttering eyes. She paces to and fro, worriedly smoking a cigarette.

"He's dangerous," she says. "Trouble. A fuckup." She takes a draw from her cigarette, sucking it to ash and embers with a single long pull. "He's an addict. You should talk to him, Christian. You know what he's like." She produces another cigarette from nowhere. It's already lit. "It would be best for the band, for both of us, if he were gone, right? You're with me on this, right, Christian?"

She looks at you as if expecting you to speak. You don't. She continues, repeating everything she's said before, like an endless loop recording. She pauses in the same places to smoke her cigarette. She makes eye contact in all the same moments.

You puzzle over this pattern, this Erin of the automations, realize that there's something more, words unsaid floating through the air. *I can't do this anymore*, Erin seems to say. *I'm in too deep. I need an excuse, an escape. I need an alibi.* Her eyes are pleading. *Give me an out,*

Christian. Give me a way. Then she, too, is gone.

Your pattern shifts, driven along on bass and high hat, the floor tom adding resonance and filling the gaps. The next apparition is Robbie Snow, wearing the same vicious, half-drunk grimace as he did that night at the Smoking Monkey. It's Robbie, alright, but his eyes are black and empty holes. He bares his teeth, sharp and dangerous, swinging ironclad fists at you, intent on pummeling you to mash. Steam erupts from his ears like a cartoon locomotive.

When he makes contact, it knocks you backward into the bar. You turn back to face him, but he has become a wall of flailing fists, each one connecting, driving you back down, driving you into the earth itself.

Blood streams from your face—bits of bone, stray teeth, floating along in its debris-choked floodwaters. There is no pain, you realize, only the illusion of rent and tattered flesh, only the illusion of your adversary, your enemy, your dissembler.

"Enough," you choke, spitting blood and gore into his face. "Enough." He pulls back, uncertain. You drip from his hand, his face.

Your pattern reaches its climax, its apex, the build of sound and drums and beat infusing all. The gods stand ready, lining the walls of the practice space, the goat god behind you, hands upon your shoulders. Your hands are a blur. This is the fastest you have ever played, the most accurate rhythm you have ever found. This is the beat of stillborn stars, of seabottom vents, of atoms fucking in the dark. You glare at Robbie Snow, bring down your stick against the crash cymbal. He shatters as you hit, shards falling to the floor and disappearing.

You set down your sticks, crossed atop the snare. Your hands, your arms, your shoulders ache. Inside your chest, your heart pounds staccato, excited from the grand excursion. You pick up a rag, an old T-shirt from the floor and mop at your sweat-covered face. You breathe, listening to your pulse, your breath as it slows to normal.

The door opens, ushering sunlight into the room. Danny Zee, guitarist and singer for Sinister Without Smiles, is standing there. "What the fuck was that?" he calls. "I could hear you all the way across the lot. Hell, I could feel you, too. What the fuck kind of beat was that?"

You look up at him, grin your damaged grin. He looks around. "You been sleeping in here, Christian?" You stand up, still catching your breath, then pick your sticks up off the snare. The tip of one, you notice, is starting to splinter, its tip sharp, dangerous. Danny shrugs. "I don't care if you do, once in a while. I've done it myself. Just don't get caught, okay?"

You nod. He continues, "Check it, I met up with those two faggots from Shithaüs, right? Those fuckers managed to pull an opening spot for fucking Occam's Switchblade next weekend. Big surprise show, some battle-of-the-bands showcase. They got a new bass player or some shit. I heard it's that asshole from your old band." He reaches back toward the small of his back. "Anyway, you know that old, fucked-up UniVibe pedal they been bugging me about? Well, check this out." He pulls out an object—small, steel grey, just larger than his hand—from where it was tucked into his waistband. "Look what those Nazi faggot fucks swapped me for it. It's a fucking Parabellum. Otto said it was his granddad's. You know what that means." You step forward, your sticks clutched in your hands, the whole one in your left, the sharp and broken one in your right.

"This thing's got to be worth what, six, eight hundred bucks, easy, right?" Danny starts to tuck the pistol back into his pants, turning his back to you as he does so, changes his mind. He holds it at arm's length, aiming out the open door at a scraggly cat that pauses in the act of walking past to scratch an ear. "It's loaded, too," he says, his neck, his back exposed. "Pop, pop," he says, pulling back his hand to imitate recoil. "I wonder if it ever killed anybody?"

You tighten your grip on the drumstick in your right hand, staring at the thin blue line stretching up and down beneath the skin of his neck. Means to an end, you think, then thrust and bury the tip of the stick in his skin, severing the blue-veined highway. He gasps, gurgles, dropping the pistol to the ground with a clatter. You drag Danny inside, then return to pick up and examine the pistol, thinking of Robbie.

TRACK 11
RADIO, RADIO

Terrri is straddling me, shaking me, when I awaken. At first, I think it's foreplay, rough foreplay, sure, but that's not unheard of, given the last couple of months. Then I realize what she's saying. "Wake up, you cocksucker, wake the fuck up." Terrri's got her hands on my shoulders, gripping tight. "Your little ex-girlfriend is on the radio."

My few remaining fragments of a pleasant dream turn to ash and blow away as I push back, force my way up onto my elbows. Terrri still straddles me, skin pressing hard against mine, kissing close, intimate. I tilt my lips toward hers, attempting to steal a morning kiss. She rebuffs me. "Would you be serious for just two fucking minutes and listen?"

I do, turning to face the radio once I realize what's playing. As if seeing would make a difference. It's a stripped-down version of Heroes for Goats' "A Killing." Erin's anthem. No drums, just a pair of acoustic guitars, Erin's unmistakable voice, and a male vocal adding harmony. The song builds, builds, but instead of the crashing electric cacophony of our original arrangement, it assumes near sacred proportions, ancient plainsong. Nothing but Erin Locke, her mysterious partner, the resonance of wood and strings, and the sound of an echoing hall. The song is breathtaking.

I sit in silence, listening, forgetting all about the close proximity of Terrri Terrrors, conscious only of the naked honesty infusing Erin's voice. Two minutes pass and the song ends, carried out by an intimate round of applause. I blink, becoming once again aware of my surroundings, of Terrri's body touching mine. "Wow," I say. "Just wow. That was one hell of a version."

Terrri shoves me back onto the bed, anger in her eyes. The DJ, that morning girl with the fake British accent, comes on. "You 'eard it 'ere first," she announces. "That was Erin Locke featuring Paulie Gray on the acoustic version of 'A Killing,' recorded right 'ere in our Studio Space. I'm going to play some commercials, pay some bills, but when we get back, I've got an exclusive interview with Erin. She'll be talking about the end of Heroes for Goats, her new start with The Paulie Gray Band, and their new record on Leviathan... right after this..." An ad for one of the local car dealerships, the one with the monkey, replaces the DJ, offering unprecedented close-out deals on last year's models. I smile at Terrri.

"Don't," she says. "I'm in no mood."

I turn my grin into an exaggerated frown, making sure to thrust out my lower lip in a mock pout. Terrri can't help but smile briefly, but quickly regains her composure. "Cut it out," she says. "I'm trying to be serious here."

I exhale sharply. "Okay," I say. "What's wrong?"

"It's her," says Terrri after a few moments' pause. She looks down, evading my eyes. "I know you've still got a thing for her. Don't you?"

"Wait," I say. "What? Me? Erin?" Terrri looks up at me with gold-flecked green eyes, meeting my line of sight as if for the first time. "Where did this come from?"

"Yeah," she says. "I can tell. You still dream of fucking her. She's what you really want. Isn't she? Not like this." Terrri sweeps her hand alongside the line of her body, a flourish apparently intended to draw attention to her flaws, her imperfections. "She's real," she says. "Not a freak like me."

I push myself back up onto my elbows, untangling my legs from Terrri's. "You're jealous?" I ask.

She crosses her arms, looks down her nose at me. "You blame me?" she asks. "Admit it," she adds, shaking her head. "You still think of her."

I've had enough of Terrri's line of questioning, knowing that it's an unwinnable challenge. So I take advantage of her crossed arms, springing up and suddenly pushing her down onto the bed, effectively reversing our positions, pressing my body between her legs. I tilt my head down, kissing her forehead. "So what if I do?" I ask. "You're the one I'm with."

She starts to reply, but I interrupt her, pressing my mouth to hers, a crush of lips, an entangling of tongues, of teeth. I feel my prick stirring, pressing against her through the bedsheets. I nuzzle at her neck, feel her warm breath against the side of my face. I explore the contours of her body with my hands, running my fingertips along the surface of her skin. I kiss her breasts, exploring the subtle scars under each with my thumbs as I take each nipple in turn between my lips, my teeth. She takes my face into her hands and draws me back up to hers, kissing me, deep and hard. "I want you," she gasps. "I want you to pretend I'm her."

"The fuck?" I demand. "You can't be serious."

"Dead serious," she says, and I can tell by the expression on her face that she is. "I want you," she says, running a finger along my lower lip, sliding it into my mouth. "To act like I'm Erin." She affects a campy approximation of Erin's voice. "I'm Erin Locke, the Queen of Rock," says Terrri. "And I want you to fuck me, Robbie Snow."

"Jesus, Terrri," I say.

"Call me Erin, Robbie," she demands, wrestling me to the bed and mounting me.

"Jesus, Erin," I reply.

Terrri presses her open mouth to mine, probing and exploring it with her tongue. We share a common breath, she exhales, I inhale. I exhale, she inhales, a circular serpent's flow, tongue-tied and tantalized. After what seems an eternity, she releases me and begins to make her way down my body, kissing my chin, my throat, my chest.

"Terrri..." I say. She sinks her teeth into my left nipple, biting hard enough to break my skin. I wince, looking up at her. A trickle of blood reddens her lips.

"I'm Erin now," insists Terrri. "I'm the Queen of Rock." She dabs at my bleeding skin with a finger, traces arcane symbols on my skin. "Don't make that mistake again," she says, leaning back down and lapping at the wound. "Or I'll fucking kill you."

"Okay," I gasp as she moves down my torso, kissing and nibbling her way down my body.

"Okay what?" she asks, arriving at my hips and pulling down the sheet to expose my erect prick, which she takes in hand and kisses. Terrri bares her teeth at me.

"Okay... Erin," I say, feeling as if it's my life in her hands. I close my eyes, listening to Erin Locke talk on the radio about major label contracts, tour plans, and the tender and remarkable Paulie Gray, as Terrri takes me into her mouth. I twist my body, grasp her hair with my fingertips, murmuring "Oh Erin," like she wants, like she imagines she needs.

XXX

Later that night, we find ourselves knocking back a few post-practice pints at the Dresden Room with Johnny Rainbow and Maxxy Blue, making big plans for the coming weekend's show, a surprise appearance at Madame Sook's Pleasure Palace.

"So it's all set, right?" asks Terrri, rubbing my leg with her foot under the table.

"We're the last act on," says Johnny, "Eleven o'clock stage time. And since it's a Battle of the Bands showcase, we should have no trouble blowing everybody out of the water. Oh, and I almost forgot, we get fireworks, too." He grins. "Sook's going to break out the flashpots for us. We hit the climax, and kaboom!"

Maxxy Blue claps his hands in excitement. "They're gonna go nuts. We're gonna fucking rock it."

"Don't we always?" asks Terrri, migrating her foot up my leg and teasing it against my crotch. "But I want this show to be perfect, since we're going to have a bunch of label drones in the audience. That means practice sessions tomorrow, Wednesday, and Thursday. Oh, and I want to close the gig with a cover song."

"Wait—what?" asks Johnny Rainbow, sputtering in mid-sip.

"Don't sweat it," says Terrri, affording no evidence that she's stroking my prick with her toes. "Robbie already knows the tune. We're going to do 'A Killing.'" She picks up her beer and drains it. "And," she adds, wiping her mouth, "we're going to make it our own."

"Fucking A!" exclaims Maxxy Blue.

XXX

"Christ, Terrri," I say as we begin walking back to her apartment. "What the fuck was that?"

"What the fuck was what?" asks Terrri, feigning sweetness.

"You know what," I insist. "Pretend I'm her, Robbie," I say mockingly. "Wanting to do her song. What the fuck is up with that?"

Terrri stops and puts her hands on her hips defiantly. "You have a problem with my decision?" Cars rush past, their strobing headlights casting flickering gigantic shadows against the wall behind us.

"It's not the song," I insist. "It's a good song. It's getting radio. Hell, I co-wrote the damn thing. It's this cruel game of you pretending to be Erin. It's fucked up."

Terrri looks down at the ground, twisting the toe of a high-heeled foot as she does so. She does this for a few moments, wordlessly, then looks back up at me, hope in her eyes. "So you're sure it's me you want? Not Erin?" she asks.

"God, no," I say, reaching out my hand and taking hers. "I mean sure, once upon a time I had it pretty bad for Erin, but that was months ago." I pull her close and touch the side of her cheek with my fingertips. "Before you."

Even in the dim and erratic light, I can see the blush on Terrri's face, so I slide my arm around her waist and start walking her along, back on track to her place. "Are you sure?" she asks eventually. "I mean she's, well, real." Terrri stops again, takes both of my hands in hers, and looks into my eyes. "She's real and I'm all artifice, all illusion."

"Terrri," I say. "All women are magicians. Ninety-nine percent of sex is about illusion. You're my girl. I want you." We start walking again, and I feel pretty proud of myself, aroused even, because I said something so deep it echoes. "Come on," I suggest. "Let's get home. This neighborhood sucks."

We walk along, my right arm around her waist, her left hand thrust into the back pocket of my jeans, her head against my shoulder. After a few moments of walking, she looks up at me. "Prove it," she says. "Kiss me."

I look around, making sure the coast is clear. "I'll do more than kiss you, Terrri," I say, pushing her into the shielded doorway of a closed hardware store, against a silvered window framing an unlit neon open sign. A trickle of yellow light spills out from the counter through the windows, doors, accented every few seconds by a flashing blue light from the store's security system. I press my mouth against hers, kissing her as hard as I can manage, my hands holding, steadying her head.

I press against her, exploring the curves of her body, the contours of her clothing, with my fingertips. "Oh God, Oh God, Robbie," she pants. "I want you. I want your cock in my mouth."

She starts to slide down the surface of the window, but I stop her, press her back against it. "No," I say, pulling her back up and kissing her again, then dropping to my knees before her, pushing up her skirt.

"Stop," gasps Terrri, but I've already pulled back her panties, taken her into my own mouth. She runs her fingers through my hair as I explore every inch of her with my lips, my teeth, my tongue. "Oh Robbie," she whispers over the noise of passing traffic. "Oh, Robbie."

Terrri's breathing quickens, becoming irregular as her climax draws near. But she stops me, pushing me away. "Quit, Robbie, quit," she says. "We've got company."

It takes me a few moments to adjust to this new information, moments filled with Terrri adjusting her skirt and me looking up into her confused and frightened face. When I finally look over my shoulder, a man's voice speaks, mean and nasal. "Looks like we found a couple of faggots, boys." He steps into the light. He's young, muscular. His head is shaved. He wears a white sleeveless T-shirt, a wife-beater, which exposes his tattoos, variations on the Solar Cross and the number eighty eight, to the cold night air. His jeans, rolled at the bottoms to expose big, black, steel-toed boots, are held up with suspenders.

Behind him, two similarly-attired men laugh, as if the first has cracked a particularly clever joke. "We don't like faggots in our neighborhood," says one, cracking his knuckles.

"Shit," whispers Terrri under her breath. "Skinheads."

"Look," I say, working my way to my feet. "We'll just be going then, okay?" I step in front of Terrri and reach back for her hand. "We don't want any trouble."

"Should have thought of that earlier, fag," says the first skinhead, shoving me, his palm against my shoulder. "Shouldn't you?" Behind him, Tweedle Dumbshit and Tweedle Dipshit just keep laughing. Terrri takes my hand, and I can feel her shaking.

XXX

Now don't get me wrong. I've been in plenty of fights in my life. You can't grow up in Garageland without finding the occasional scrap—schoolyard tussles, mostly, giving way to the inevitable band-to-band combat, fisticuffs over setlists, equipment, turf. I've never minded giving blood in order to prove a point, though it's always better to be the one on the right side of a punch. I should know—from Jesus Ramirez in the third grade to poor, dumb Christian—I've thrown plenty of them. This is different. These fuckers are out for blood.

Exactly three things are running through my mind. The first is that I don't particularly like being called a fag. Sure, Terrri's got a dick, and sure, less than five minutes earlier I had her dick in my mouth, but still. I've come to grips with it. Terrri is just Terrri, and as female as it gets. Is it too much to ask that these master race motherfuckers respect that?

The second thing to come to mind is that old adage of military strategy. Go for the big guy, the officer first. Take out the meanest motherfucker in the room and his followers will scatter. Unfortunately, this guy has a jaw like the bumper of a '57 Buick, and there's no way I'm going to be able to manage to drop him with a punch. Just thinking about it makes me ache all over, like the boots are already making contact.

The third thing I'm considering is Terrri, and how I don't want her getting her pretty face messed up on my account. We could run, but she's in heels, and that never works. Let's face it, as far as I'm concerned, the prospects are pretty dim.

And then I have an idea. Never letting go of Terrri's hand, I start to talk to those testosterone-poisoned knuckleheads, addressing the first of them, but making eye contact with the other two as well, hoping to draw them in. "Look," I say. "I know you guys are going to kick our asses from here to Timbuktu, but let me ask you a question first. You ever hear of the Sybarite Horses?" Terrri squeezes my hand.

"The fuck?" asks the first skinhead, clearly puzzled.

"Sybarite Horses. Ancient Greece. Trust me, couple of faggots," I wave, indicating Terrri and myself, "would know something about Ancient Greece, right?"

The skinheads look even more confused. "So there were these guys called the Sybarites, right? They were to cavalry what the Spartans were to infantry, dig. Big, magnificent horses, all armored, gold-plated and shit. Best spears, swords, decked out to the nines. They were unstoppable. They'd win every battle, just ride in and mop the place up."

"What's this got to do with us kicking your ass?" says the first skinhead, scratching at the stubble atop his head.

"C'mon, Jay," says Tweedle Dumbshit. "Let him finish. I want to hear this faggot out."

"Yeah," I laugh uncomfortably. "Hear the faggot out." I continue. "So this goes on for twenty, thirty years, and the Sybarites become one of the richest city-states in all Greece, dig. They start getting bored with the conquest, winning all the time, so in addition to the combat training, they start teaching the horses how to dance."

"Wait—dancing horses?" asks Tweedle Dipshit.

"That's what I said, first time I heard it," I say. "But hand to God, it's all true. They taught them how to dance.

"But cool as that sounds, that's where it starts to go wrong for the Sybarites. Check this out. These guys in a city called Croton, they find out about the dancing horses from this old, blind poet, right? They hear all about their dance steps, their moves." I let go of Terrri's hand and start dancing around in front of the skinheads. "The Crotons even manage to learn what song the Sybarites play to make the horses dance."

Maybe it's my dance moves, maybe it's the story, but I realize that the skinheads are paying attention to me, and only me, ignoring Terrri. Trying to be as subtle as possible, I motion for her to move, to start walking.

"So time comes," I continue, "that the Sybarites declare war on the Crotons, you know, 'cause they're faggots and shit, right? They ride their horses, their magnificent dancing horses right up to the city walls, ready to kick some serious ass." I notice that Terrri has slipped past me, past the skinheads, and is starting to walk away, heading toward home. The skinheads are rapt, fascinated.

"All of a sudden," I say, "every single musician in Croton stands up on the walls of the city. They've got drums, guitars, pipes, horns, accordions, the works. Somebody counts off, two, three, four, and they all start to play. And you know what they play?"

"No, what?" ask the skinheads.

"It's the Sybarite national anthem, dig? The song that gets all the horses dancing. And that's exactly what happens, all the horses start dancing. Riders start falling off, soldiers start getting trampled, shit just goes crazy." I dance around a little bit more, lifting one foot off the ground and holding my arms out to the sides. "Do you know what happens next?"

"No, what?" ask the skinheads.

"This," I shout. And with that, hard as I can, I kick the window behind me, shattering it, setting off the hardware store's burglar alarm.

Flashing lights come up, blinding. The loudest fucking bell in the world sounds, ear-splitting. The skinheads panic, run off, scattering.

I pull my boot back through the glass, chuckling, then half-run, half-limp down the street to where Terrri is waiting. She throws her arms around me as I arrive, kissing me and laughing. "My hero," she says. "You tell that story much better than I do."

Police cars speed past as we walk the rest of the way back to Terrri's apartment, lights flashing, sirens blaring, but they don't bother us. When we get inside, safe, she locks the door behind us. Terrri wrestles me onto the couch, undoing my belt and yanking my jeans down around my knees in the process. She tears off her panties, tossing them into a corner, climbs atop me, covering my face with kisses. "My hero," she repeats. "I have a reward for you."

As Terrri Terrrors mounts me, as she writhes and pants and moans atop me, the radio, still on, plays "A Killing." I think of Erin Locke, of Terrri Terrrors, of a dozen different girls. But mostly, I think of the Queen of Rock, and know, no matter what face, what body she wears, I cannot help but be her loyal subject.

INTERLUDE #3

She's Erin Locke, the Queen of Rock. She climbs into the bus. She glances over her shoulder as she boards, looking back at the rising sun, at the backlit roadies loading equipment, amplifiers, enough musical materiel to fight a war into the trucks. She steps up into the plush interior, notes the crush of carpet beneath her boots, runs her fingers along the edge of red velour-covered seats.

The rest of the band is already aboard with Paulie sitting among them, holding court, a traveling poet-warrior among his retainers. Jimmy Bock, the drummer, sits on Paulie's left, drinking a morning beer, laughing at Paulie's jokes. Dalton Ryan, the stunt guitarist, and Parker Harrison, the keyboard player, a pair of chattering Walkman headphones around his neck, sit on Paulie's right.

It's been a month and a half of getting to know these guys, thinks Erin, their timing, their styles, their skills, and yet, she's not so sure she knows them after all. Seven weeks on the road, seven weeks of sharing space, should change all that.

"Erin," calls Paulie, standing as she steps onboard. He strides across to her, guides her over to the guys, arm around her waist. She settles in between Paulie and Jimmy, stifling a yawn with a hand held over her mouth.

"Too early for you?" jokes Dalton, cracking open a beercan.

"Yeah," says Erin, feeling another yawn brewing in her lungs. "This getting up at sunrise stuff is new to me, though I've seen plenty from the other end."

"You'll get used to it," says Dalton. "And sleeping on the bus, and bad road food, the works." He takes a sip of his beer, then remembers his manners. "Get you one?" he offers, reaching into the cooler beside him and removing a sweating can. "It'll help you sleep."

Erin accepts the can and opens it. She drinks, washing down the morning funk with the watery, metallic brew. "So, what now?" asks Erin.

"We wait for Captain Crash," says Paulie. "And then we hit the road."

"Captain Crash?"

"Our driver. He's done our last three tours," volunteers Paulie.

"Used to drive Blue Öyster Cult around," adds Dalton.

"Not really the kind of name that inspires confidence, is it?" asks Erin.

The guys laugh at this, but nobody reassures Erin. Instead, they joke, drink beer, smoke cigarettes, and claim seats and couches in preparation for the long drive ahead.

Erin settles back into a window seat on the right side of the bus, after Parker shows her to the band's collective cache of Walkmans, tapes, and entertainment devices. With the binaural bombast of Lou Reed's *The Bells* playing in her ears, Erin watches as the trucks are loaded. As the crew that will move The Paulie Gray Band from city to city mobilizes, maneuvers, Erin pulls a small notebook and pen from her jacket pocket and begins to sketch pictures of mermaids.

Soon, the engine of the bus rumbles to life, surprising Erin with its sudden vibration. She glances around, "Disco Mystic" sounding through her headphones. A few more people have boarded the bus. There's the driver, sixty-something and bearded in a black sailor's cap, his blue eyes reflecting in the rear view mirror. Further back, Alvin Ashe, the road manager, and one of the label zombies—is it Sturm or Drang?—are chatting with Paulie, making plans. Sturm, Erin decides, holds his ever-present clipboard in hand.

The bus lurches forward, beginning to work its way toward the freeway, just one part of the convoy column. The other label rep— definitely Drang—sits down next to Erin, grinning. Erin politely pulls back her headphones.

"Are you writing the next big hit?" he asks, pointing to the notebook in her lap.

Erin laughs courteously. "Probably not," she ventures. "But who knows?" She closes the notebook.

Drang glances around. "Do you like the bus?" he asks.

"It's okay," replies Erin. "Better than doing the driving and loading by myself, I guess." She thinks of the previous summer, of the shows Heroes for Goats played in LA, Phoenix, Tempe, and Las Vegas, of Robbie and Christian, the three of them crammed into the sputtering Volkswagen along with all their equipment. She remembers Christian, in the passenger seat, tapping out rhythms against the dashboard with his sticks, the side-view mirror serving as a surrogate ride cymbal. She remembers Robbie, sharing driving duties as she slept in the backseat, a bag of effects pedals serving as her pillow, and how he sang along with David Bowie's *Hunky Dory* as it blared from the ghetto blaster. Good times, gone too soon. She wonders what's become of Christian and Robbie, then realizes that Drang has been talking.

"...radio response like that, Erin," he says. "It's remarkable, really. The song seems to have captured the zeitgeist."

"Wait, what?" asks Erin. "What's a shite heist?"

"Zeitgeist," he says. "The Spirit of the Age. We should talk, Erin. About the future. Not now, of course." He looks around, as if making sure the coast is clear. "In a week or so. Let us buy you a drink or two, talk about what our organization might be able to do for you. Who knows, you may want to consider a solo career." He reaches into the breast pocket of his suit jacket, pulls forth an off-white business card. Drang sets the card down, face up, on top of Erin's notebook. The Leviathan Records logo, metallic and red, sparkles up at Erin. "Don't hesitate to call, Erin," he says. "If you need anything at all. Anything."

Erin takes the card, slides it between the pages of her book. "I'll think about it," she says. "But right now, shhh." She holds a finger in front of her lips, shushing him, pulls the headphones back over her ears. "Lou Reed's on."

TRACK 12
JENNIFER ARMY

A blue ghost of smoke dances across Jennifer's lips, spreads itself thin, then dissipates into the night through the half-open driver's window of the pickup. Jennifer drums the fingers of her left hand against the hard plastic steering wheel, matching time with the outro of Stevie Wonder's "Ordinary Pain" as it plays through the truck's antiquated 8-Track stereo. She keeps perfect time even though the cacophonic sixteenth-note assault that spills from Madame Sook's Pleasure Palace into the gravel parking lot threatens to bury Stevie and the rest of the world in unwelcome noise. Jennifer turns to face the passenger seat, then offers Jen the spliff smoldering between her right thumb and index finger. Jen doesn't take it. Instead, she stares out the open passenger window, oblivious, drifting. The 8-Track deck squeaks, changes programs with a clunk. With a sweet choral coo, "Love's In the Need of Love Today" begins to play.

"Hey, Stoner," interrupts Jennifer, "Your turn on the swingset."

"Huh?" starts Jen. "Oh, thanks." She takes the joint between left thumb and forefinger, brushing the side of Jennifer's hand as she draws it to her own mouth. Jen takes a hit, then glances down toward the floor to the empty beer bottles at her feet.

"What were you thinking?" asks Jennifer.

"I was pretending I was one of those girls on the mudflaps of a cross-country rig," she exhaled. "I'd be all sleek and sexy and silver. I'd travel from coast to coast. I wouldn't have a care in the world."

Jen glances back up. Their eyes meet, hold, explore. Jen smiles, hands the joint back to Jennifer, turns again to look out her window. Overhead, atop the brick building opposite Madame Sook's, a billboard screams "Real men don't use porn." Beneath it, a rebuttal is scrawled in Krylon orange metal-flake: "That's why they have daughters." The billboard's old, it's been here forever. Rumor has it Erin Locke climbed up and drunkenly tagged it after the first time Heroes for Goats played Madame Sook's. That was a year ago and now they're on the radio. They've hit the big time. Jen wonders whether Jennifer Army has the fortitude to do the same. Above it all, the moon performs an elegant striptease behind seven veiled wisps of purple cloud. A single streetlight struggles to illuminate the parking lot.

Inside Madame Sook's, Shithaüs launches into the guitar feedback and drum machine assault of their third song, only distinguishable from the first two by the eight-second gap between them. Jen imagines Madame Sook behind the bar, pacing like a puffed-up Korean mother hen, serving up cheap watery beer to the chattering smoking masses who fill the tiny nightclub. On the truck's 8-Track, Little Stevie Wonder warbles every possible permutation of the letters of the word love. "Love. L-O-V-E. Love."

Jennifer breaks the moment. "You are so stoned," she laughs.

XXX

Twenty-three minutes ago, Jennifer Army finished their set at Madame Sook's Pleasure Palace in a crescendo of harmonious power and discordant fury. They blew the place apart, playing hard and fast and spot-on dangerous. They were tight, the tightest they'd ever been, and when Jenna shattered that cheap Mexican pawnshop Strat against the edge of the stage, the crowd went batshit, complete with rabid fans diving for pieces, sacred relics. As the feedback died, Jenni thrust one hand in the air, throwing the crowd the goat, then husked into her microphone, "Thanks, we're called Jennifer Army, and you guys fuckin' rock." The crowd went wild. Jennifer, behind the drums, glanced over at Jen on bass. "No, you fuckin' rock," she mouthed. Somebody killed the spotlights, and for a moment there was nothing to the world but blackness, sweat, and heat. Then the house lights came on.

XXX

Seventeen minutes ago, Jennifer Army finished stripping down their equipment, throwing cables, cords, and pedals into milk crates. Jenna stacked amps onto a waiting hand truck. Jennifer packed her drums into road cases while Jen wiped the strings of her bass with a rag and began to zip it into its case. Jenni took turns flipping back her feathered blond hair, chatting with fans, and pimping shirts, stickers, and CDs.

Jennifer watched as a young man approached the edge of the stage. She'd noticed him in the crowd at the last handful of shows, always staring at Jen. He didn't belong. He was dull, square, all glasses and acne in a blue-checked button-down shirt. He pointed at Jen. "You're p-pretty good," he stammered. "Are all f-four of you really named J-Jennifer?"

Jen turned to look, and started to say something, but Jennifer beat her to it. "She's not interested, sucker. You ain't her type. She's a dyke." She threw one arm around Jen and clutched her close, possessively, then motioned menacingly toward the man with her drumsticks. The young man glanced down at his brown oxford shoes, turned and wandered away.

"What'd you do that for?" demanded Jen, giving her bandmate a shove. "He looked harmless."

"He looked like a serial killer. I'm just watching out for you. Suit yourself, go ahead, take off with some random dillrod. Just don't say I didn't warn you when he's eating your gizzard." She chomped and snatched at Jen's waist menacingly, inducing fits of laughter.

XXX

Twelve minutes ago, three-fourths of Jennifer Army finished loading the equipment into the pickup. It was a beat-to-shit Ford 100, an old farm truck, at one time dark blue, but currently rust red. Jen had paid a hundred and fifty bucks for it. Jenni, as usual, stayed inside to schmooze. They covered the gear with a green plastic tarp. "Look," Jenna said, "I'm splitting." She rubbed her right wrist as she spoke. "You two figure out which one's pulling guard duty." Before she turned to leave she added, "Hey, we straight-up rocked tonight. We killed 'em." The two girls nodded in response. "I'll see you at the space," added Jenna, then she disappeared into the night, leaving Jennifer and Jen to run through rounds of Ro-Sham-Bo for in-and-out privileges, best two out of three.

XXX

Ten minutes ago, Jen sat atop the cab of her pickup, dangling her boots into the bed, alone in the parking lot. She listened as the second band, a drum-machined duo called Shithaüs, hit the stage. She quickly decided that they were one of the worst bands, if not the worst band, she'd ever heard. Off-key, off-time, off-color lyrics wafted through the air, noisome as an unwelcome fart. Jen wondered if Madame Sook was planning to pull the plug on the dissonant diatribe, knowing that bad music made the patrons less thirsty. It was at that point that Jen decided the night and the winner-take-all cash prize from this week's Rock and Roll Showdown was in the bag. Moments later, however, all bets were off, as Jennifer returned with dire news of who was closing the show.

"Fucking Occam's Switchblade," lamented Jennifer. She bounced on the balls of her feet, like a pugilist ready to punch someone. "It isn't fair. Cheesy fucking glam-rock faggots. I mean they're fucking professionals, they're signed, made. What do they think they're doing, coming down here, slumming our scene? I don't care if they're trying out a new bassist, this Showdown was ours. We deserve the glory, the freakin' money. That crowd was ours. Fuck Madame Sook. She's nothing but a lying, cheating, no-good douchebag. Bitch set us up."

"Calm down," replied Jen. "We'll chalk it up to practice. At least we didn't have to pay to play." Jen tried her damnedest to feign cool, to project unflappable, even though she wasn't sure it worked. "How'd Jenni take it?"

"Jenni's gone. She sold a few shirts, then she bailed with some mohawk guy."

"So, you wanna take off? Head back to the practice space?"

"Nah. Not yet. If you're cool, I'm going back in to check out the rest of Shithaüs's set. It's like a car crash. Get you anything?"

"I could use a beer."

"Ask and ye shall receive," said Jennifer as she pulled a bottle from one of the inside pockets of her black trenchcoat. "Hey look," she demonstrated, "I've got the coat of many beers. I nipped them while Sook was yelling at some fat kid." She popped the twist cap, dropped it on the ground, handed the sweating brown bottle up to Jen.

"Thanks," Jen smiled. "So, are you planning on sticking around for Occam's Switchblade?"

"I dunno. They're such a freak show." She looked down, twisted one pointed boot into the gravel, then looked back up, beaming. "I know. Maybe we stick around long enough to kidnap their singer. Then Madame Sook would have to let us win. Besides, what are they going to do if Terrri Terrrors turns up missing, stick a picture of him on a carton of half-and-half?"

Jen laughed at this. She glanced over the club, then back at Jennifer. A beat-up white van was pulling into the parking lot, grinding gravel beneath its tires. Its headlights were off. She pulled a swig from her beer. "Hey, J. I got a J. You wanna get toasty?"

XXX

Jennifer touches the back of Jen's hand with hers, then takes the joint. "My turn." She pulls a hit, offers it back to Jen, who declines. Jennifer crushes the coal carefully against the pitted chrome bracket of the side-view mirror, then drops the blunted roach into the ashtray. "I'm headed back in," she exhales. "I wanna see if Sook gives these cheeseballs the boot. But I'll be back. You cool?"

"Yeah," replies Jen. "I'm cool."

Jennifer opens the truck door and steps out into the night. "Hey, J," she calls back through the open door. "I picked up a flyer. Annie Aronburg's playing over at Lipstick on Thursday night. You wanna go check it out?"

"Nah, I'm not so into acoustic and angry this week," answers Jen, as she crosses her arms, cold.

"Yeah, me neither," says Jennifer. She looks down, shuts the door of the truck with a thud, turns, and begins walking across the gravel lot back toward the bar, hands thrust into her pockets. She walks past a woman and man sitting on the bumper of the double-parked white van, sharing a cigarette, and nods a casual greeting. Back in the truck, Stevie Wonder climaxes into a chorus: "When you feel your life's too hard," he sways, "Just go have a talk with God." Onstage in Madame Sook's Pleasure Palace, Shithaüs pauses, then launches into another ground-glass guitar and drum machine attack which only increases in volume as Jennifer reaches the nightclub's door and disappears into the crowd.

Jen stares out her window up toward the now-naked moon. She watches as a shooting star streaks across the moon's face, whispers her silent wish, turns up Stevie Wonder, hoping to drown the outside world in music.

TRACK 13
A KILLING

"One, please," you say as you press a crumpled, blood-flecked ten-spot into the hand of the girl at the door. She holds it aloft, checking it against the cool luminescence of the lamp clipped to the edge of her table. She smacks her gum, tucks the bill under her money drawer, motioning you forward.

"Which band?" she asks, bored, by rote, as if she's asked this question a hundred times this evening. She probably has, you realize.

"What?" you ask.

"Which band are you here to see?" She's plainly impatient. "Which band, or no band."

You glance at the evening's flyer, thumbtacked to the doorjamb at eye level. Battle of the Bands. Jennifer Army. Shithaüs. Special Guest. "Shithaüs," you say.

"They just went on," she says, over the din, scratching a mark onto a clipboard with her pencil. You are one of only five marks for Shithaüs, squeezed between a couple dozen for Jennifer Army and more than a hundred for Special Guest. It isn't much of a secret.

You raise your arms as the bouncer, a forty-year-old punk rocker with a bleached Mohawk, efficiently pats down your sides. "Go ahead," he nods. He doesn't think to check the small of your back. They never do, so your pistol remains hidden, tucked into the waistband of your jeans. You go in, buy a beer, and wait.

We take the stage like we're storming a beach, pushing our way past Shithaüs before they've even had a chance to strip down all their gear. Devlin Deck shoves the hand truck holding his amp and one of his cabinets along at full speed, practically running down the members of Shithaüs as he wheels it onto the stage. When he returns with the second cabinet, he damn near does it again. There's an enviable epitaph: mashed by a Marshall stack. Maxxy Blue follows, hauling the cases containing his drums, begins the task of removing each ebony and bone-colored piece, assembling the set with the deft accuracy of a blindfolded sniper.

It takes Johnny Rainbow all of three seconds to hook up his keyboards, so he serenades us with a short burst of Bach's "Tocatta and Fugue," his way of testing the setup. I plug in my amp, connect my effects pedal, wireless unit, and bass, crank up the volume. I tune to Devlin's A, watching as Johnny Rainbow adjusts Terrri's microphone, calling "check, check" into its diaphragm. Satisfied, I pull three seven-day glass Jesus candles, eyes cut out, from my bag, lighting them as I set them atop my amplifier. Backstage, though I can't see her, I know Terrri is putting the finishing touches on her makeup and costume in the tiny storage closet Madame Sook let her use as a dressing room. Devlin, Maxxy, Johnny, and I face the curtain, instruments cradled like weapons in our hands, listening to the house music, David Bowie's *Diamond Dogs*, as it underscores the restless breathing of the crowd.

I glance over to Devlin, his eyes closed, a look of intense concentration on his mascara-accented lids, a murmured mantra animating his lipsticked lips. Johnny and Maxxy share a private joke, laughing as they run through their own last-minute rituals. I think of Terrri, of doing lines and kissing her in the back of the van, not much more than an hour earlier as we waited for our turn on stage. I can still taste her on my tongue.

Madame Sook bustles onto the stage, the full moon of her face showing signs of exertion through its thick veneer of makeup. "She say she almost ready," clucks Sook, pressing a remote control into Johnny's hands. It looks like the control for a toy racecar. "You start now. You play. Last song come, push red button. Give you big, big boom. Now I go open curtain." She waddles off, leaving behind a bottle of beer for each of us.

"You heard the lady," calls Johnny Rainbow, chuckling at Sook's brusque manner. "Everybody ready to rock?" We each nod, in turn. Maxxy holds his sticks aloft in the air, tapping them together to count us in.

Our opening salvo is an instrumental, "The Motherfucker March," a creeping, grinding bit of striptease. I walk my fingers up and down the frets of my bass, following the stuttering percussion from Maxxy Blue. Johnny Rainbow's keys produce an unholy racket, like James Brown's horns, the Robert Shaw Chorale, and the sound of marching boots run through a meat grinder.

The curtain parts, bathing us in red-filtered light, like Hell's own orchestra. Center stage, Devlin Deck pumps his hips as he strokes the phallus of his guitar, his fingers a blur of power chords and death-defying wheedly-deedlies. I look out into the darkling crowd, affecting a feral grimace and tossing back my hair. I can't make out any details—it's impossible with the stage lights' glare—but I know to feign eye contact, to give the kids that sensation that I'm looking right at them, through them.

We bring the song to a head, letting the "Woah-eh-oh" sample from Johnny's keyboard take precedence, prolonging it enough that the audience feels compelled to chant along. We build, then break, the spotlights cutting off just as all pretense of melody and harmony gives way to an inchoate growl. Devlin kneels before his amplifiers, inducing a screech of feedback resembling nothing heard since giant lizards stomped across the surface of a young, green earth. The sound decays, and the room goes black. At center stage, a single spotlight bursts into brightness, illuminating the hourglass form of Terrri Terrrors, dressed in skintight black vinyl and eight-inch thigh-high platform boots, towering above the band.

Terrri takes the microphone between her hands. She runs her fingers along its shaft, caressing it, down the arm of the stand and back up again. She flicks her tongue at its head, then clutches the mic in her right hand, wrenching it from the stand. Leaning forward, she raises her left fist into the air, saluting the crowd. They go wild.

Terrri pulls her arm back down, cradling the mic in both hands, as we slide into "Hey Jo," a crazed cabaret version of the blues standard, framing Jocasta's tragic story. "The offspring never killed the tyrant father," sings Terrri. "And would it really matter if he struck the fucker down?"

Without pause, we launch into "The Gynosphinx and the Organ Grinders," a straight-up rocker with a shimmy and a stomp. Terrri pouts and prances for the crowd, a slinking feline, graceful and grotesque. As Devlin Deck tears into one of his trademark blistering solos, Terrri preens, pretending to lap at her paws, brushing back her long black hair as she purrs.

Terrri disappears during the instrumental "Slaughtersphere," a chaotic, lurching cacophony, while Devlin and I trade dueling lines and phrases. He shudders out a series of semitones that I must push my fingers into overdrive to counter. Somehow, I manage to keep up, though I know that I am relying on his virtuosity to make me seem like a better musician than I am. Devlin drops to his knees, acting as if I have somehow bested him in hand-to-hand swordplay. I slap and pop the last few notes of the funk bassline, then hold my axe aloft as Johnny's keyboards burst into a sped-up choral anthem, driven by Maxxy's alternating bass and floor toms.

Terrri reappears, changing from dominatrix decadence to a shimmering green floor-length gown, but keeping the elbow-length gloves and platform boots from her previous ensemble. We slow it down for a ballad called "Silver-Frosted Mother Love," that shows off the full range of Terrri's countertenor voice, then bring up the tempo for "Police and Thebes" and "Overwrought with Fancies." Near the climax, Terrri strips off her gloves, one at a time, draping the first around Devlin's neck and the second around mine.

For "Whoracles and Other Liars," Terrri is backed only by Johnny Rainbow's tinny honky-tonk piano while the rest of us take a quick break, drinking our beers and mopping sweat off our faces. We return with another instrumental, "Lost and Damned," featuring one of Devlin Deck's epic mountaintop guitar solos. His slithering fingers defy every natural law as they force his Gibson SG to perform unimaginable feats. Somewhere in the middle of the number, Madame Sook turns on the smoke machines, filling the stage with clouds of cascading vapor.

As Devlin's last note rings out, the stage lights go dark. I feel Terrri brush past me, touching my face with her fingertips as she crosses the stage. "Oh, yeah," she whispers. "You're on fire tonight."

When the spotlight comes up again, Terrri is completely shrouded in mist and mystery, her voice alone, barren, an a cappella opening to the next tune, "Fruit of Luckless Misbegetting." She sings the first four bars alone, then each of us in turn comes in, measure by measure—a warm pad from Johnny's keys, a military rat-a-tat from Maxxy Blue, a walking bassline from me, a splintering surf guitar from Devlin Deck. The mist clears, revealing Terrri's latest costume, a long and veiled white wedding gown, low cut and daring enough to expose plenty of cleavage. Unabashed, she twirls and stomps about the stage, at one point placing her booted foot upon a stage front monitor and coaxing up her dress only to peel off a red lace garter, tossing it to the eager crowd.

We transition, seamlessly, into "Twice-Confounded Issue," a rollicking rave-up punctuated at its bridge by Terrri dropping to her knees before me. She clasps my hips in her hands, mock-fellating my instrument as I play, my hands stroking the neck of my bass as if enticing it to ecstasy. The crowd erupts.

We climax with "Drown Me," the last track on the record. Terrri tears her dress, rending it to rags, as she husks in haunting strains, "Will you remember what you saw? My blood spilled, breeding where you bred. Father, brother, son. Hide me away. Kill me, drown me. Ismeme, Antigone. Sobbing darlings, birthbed soiled. Drown me, drown me, depths of the sea."

She holds her hands out, arms akimbo like a sacrifice, the ruins of her dress clinging to her sweating and exposed flesh. The music reaches its crescendo, visually accented as the four firepots belch flames ten feet into the air at the edge of the stage, blasting us all with searing heat. As the audience breaks into rapturous applause, the curtains close. Terrri turns and grins at us. "Yeah, we fucking rocked."

XXX

You push your way through the crowd, toward the stage, taking advantage of your small stature to weave your way through the darkness. The smells of sweat and makeup, of spilled beer and vomit, of tobacco and marijuana smoke, fill your nostrils. Ahead of you, a drunken girl sits astride a bald man's shoulders. "Whooo!" she calls, pulling up her top and flashing her breasts to a pack of leering rogue males. A kid limps past. "Have you seen my shoe?" he asks one patron and then another. A pair of punks in wheelchairs sits at the room's perimeter, likely mosh pit casualties hanging out like forgotten ghosts on the periphery. You reach back beneath your jacket, making sure the pistol is still there, its metal cold against your skin, and then you reach the edge of the stage, the arbitrary barrier that separates performer from crowd, reveler from priest. You pull the last handful of pills from your pocket and pop them into your mouth, indifferent to what you're taking, so long as it kills the pain. The crowd begins to chant a four syllable mantra, "Occam's Switchblade, Occam's Switchblade." This will be an encore no one will soon forget.

XXX

As the crowd cries out for more, the curtains swing back open, and we file out onto the stage, one by one. First comes Maxxy Blue, then Johnny Rainbow. I'm up next, followed by Devlin Deck. We each take our positions, our instruments in hand. Maxxy counts us in, and we kick into a chugging, throbbing beat, grooving along, Devlin soloing over the pulsing rhythm.

Terrri steps out into the spotlight, the high-collared black cape wrapped around her body, accentuating her nightclub walk. When she arrives at the microphone, she takes it in hand, stalking the stage, all the while remaining covered by her cape.

"Wow, what a crowd." says Terrri, her nicotine voice a sultry purr. "You guys rock. How 'bout you give it up for the band," she prompts, motioning with her hand as applause rumbles through the hall. "As always," she continues, "we've got the incredible Devlin Deck on lead guitar." He trills, launching into a solo that would make David Gilmour jealous, his antics thrilling the crowd. "On keyboards, the incomparable Johnny Rainbow." Johnny answers Terrri's introduction with a momentary minuet, the sound of a harpsichord twisting into a chorus of demonic howls that give way to a synthesized soprano wail, sweet and pure, yet effervescent. "On drums," announces Terrri, "the fabulous Maxxy Blue." Maxxy spins his sticks, assaults his kit, pounding out a driving backbeat, stopping midway to toss both sticks into the air, then catch them again just a four count later, not missing a single beat.

"And finally," says Terrri. "The newest member of my gang. You probably know who I stole him from." She winks. "Her loss, my gain." Terrri licks her lips lasciviously. The crowd laughs. "The lovely, the talented... Robbie *fucking* Snow!"

I run my fingers up the neck of my bass, sliding into the funk groove Devlin Deck showed me just a couple weeks ago. The faux spontaneity is convincing, my fingers working like never before. I play my sixteen bars, dive back into the beat, glancing up just as the crowd erupts into applause. For a second, in the lights that sweep the crowd, I imagine I see Christian, and Erin, standing there, watching me.

"And me?" asks Terrri, pointing to herself. "Little old me?" On cue, we transition into the familiar pounding pattern that is "A Killing." "I'm Terrri Terrrors," she growls, dropping her cape to the stage, revealing a tight-fitting red, white, and blue Wonder Woman costume. "The Queen of Rock. And I'm here to make a killing."

We tear into the song, Terrri putting all the force and fury of her voice into Erin's lyrics, taking Erin's battle cry and making it her own.

It's shocking, astounding, and maybe that's why it works so well. By the first chorus, half the audience is chanting along. I think I see Christian again. By the second chorus, the whole audience has joined in, most pumping their fists along, some holding lighters in the air. As the second chorus gives way to Devlin's solo I am sure I see Christian, standing at the lip of the stage, scowling at me with hate-filled eyes.

XXX

You leap onto the stage, vaulting off the security rail, and land near the guitarist, Devlin Deck. He doesn't notice you, his eyes are closed. The gun is in your hand in seconds. You fire a shot into the air, interrupting one of those wanky, self-indulgent guitar solos that you hate so much. The guitarist stares at you, letting go of the neck of his guitar, which drops, wilting, to the stage. So much for the phallic superiority of the electric guitar.

You turn, brandishing your weapon, stalking across the stage. The audience is screaming, their jubilation turning in an instant to terror. "Robbie *fucking* Snow," you shout, firing the pistol again into the air. A spotlight explodes, sending a shower of glass fragments down, covering the stage like hailstones. The drag queen singer dives into the crowd. It's not your problem, not your target.

XXX

I duck behind my amplifier, trying to avoid Christian's gaze, but there he is, grinning wolfishly in a black hooded sweatshirt emblazoned with a Heroes for Goats patch, my artwork. He thrusts his pistol toward me, a carbon-steel extension of his arm, but holds his fire. I turn my back to him, crawl away from him on hands and knees. Johnny Rainbow picks this moment to vault from his keyboard nest, leaping to cross the stage toward escape. He doesn't make it. Christian spins and *pop*. Johnny falls back into the drum kit, sending a snare sprawling, rolling into the panicked crowd.

Broken glass punctures my hands as I scramble. Christian turns his attention back to me. "Robbie *fucking* Snow," he calls again. "Get back here, you fuckup." *Pop*, responds his pistol and the neck of my bass guitar, leaned where I left it against the amplifier, splinters, strings splaying off in all directions. The pickups hum in disarray.

"Jesus, Christian," I shout, twisting my torso to face him like a defiant insect scurrying across the hardwood stage. "Jesus."

Christian laughs, throwing back his head and grinning a ruthless, gap-toothed grimace. Oh, god of crap, I think. Did I do that? Oh, shit, I realize. I did that. "I'm sorry, Christian," I say. "Really, I'm sorry."

XXX

You level the gun, pointing it toward Robbie as he squirms before you, pathetic and scared. You wonder if he's going to piss himself before or after you kill him. "I'm sorry," he whines. "Really, I'm sorry."

You mock him. "I'm sorry, Christian," you say. "Too little, too late." You hear the rhythm of the devil drums, the voice of the goat-faced god as you stalk along the edge of the stage.

"Do it!" shout the voices. "Do it!"

"This is for Erin," you say, firing the pistol. Then there is a flash of light, a cackling, crackling of hellfire, and you know the dark gods have been appeased.

"For Erin?" I say, tasting blood, pain.

XXX

A thousand miles away, Erin Locke sits on the tour bus, chatting post-show with Heathen Heather, from the mimeographed 'zine *Punk Rawk*. "So, Erin," says Heather, brushing back her blonde bangs nervously. "What do you say to Billy Kennedy's accusation in *Music Scene*, that you're taking a step backwards by going from your own band to just being a chick bassist?"

"I just got off the phone," replies Erin. "A conference call, not more than twenty minutes ago. Me and Tina and Carol and Suzi and the Kims, just as soon as we can all find some time in our busy tour schedules, are going to come on out to LA, just so we can take turns kicking Billy's caveman ass back to the stone age." Erin smirks, lighting a cigarette.

A look of confusion migrates across Heather's face, but she takes Erin's comment in stride, moving on to the next question on her cheat sheet. "Rumor has it Heroes for Goats broke up on bad terms. Is there any bad blood between you and your old bandmates?"

"No," says Erin. "Sometimes you just have to move on. I'm sure that Robbie and Christian both understand that. They're professionals. I wish them success and happy lives."

"Really?" asks Heather.

XXX

"Oh, hell no," shouts Terrri Terrrors, storming back on stage from behind Johnny Rainbow's keyboard array. "No fucking way are you going to interrupt my show and get away with it. No fucking way are you going to do this to my band." She picks up the remote control from where it sits on Johnny's amplifier, advancing. "No fucking way, you fucking prick."

XXX

"Really," says Erin, stifling a yawn. It was a long show and she'd rather turn in, catch some shuteye, than talk to this girl. "No bad blood. It's only rock and roll. All's fair in rock and roll."

XXX

Wonder Woman is standing downstage, shouting at you, calling you a lexicon of obscene names. Between the pills' muddle and the voices, it takes you a few moments to realize that it's the drag queen, slightly mussed from her dive into the crowd, angrily advancing toward you, a black plastic box in hand. The room spins, the scent of blood fills the air, and screams mingle with echoing laughter in your ears. You look down at the pistol extending from your hand, it seems to dip and bend as you rock your hand back and forth. Behind you, Robbie Snow coughs, wounded and pathetic. He clutches at his side, blood seeping, painting his fingers.

You move to the edge of the stage, raising your unsteady arm, and pointing the pistol toward the drag queen. You squeeze off a shot. It goes wild, puncturing the grille and paper cone of an amplifier. Wonder Woman steps closer, stalking toward you, anger in her eyes. You level the pistol again, pulling the trigger, but nothing happens.

You pull the trigger again. Nothing happens. You look down the length of the pistol, noticing that your view of the sight is blocked by the toggle, which juts upward at an odd angle. You pull the trigger again. Nothing.

"No fucking way," yells Wonder Woman, jabbing at the object in her hands with her fingertips. "No fucking way do you fuck with the Queen of Rock."

Suddenly, the world is a rush of wings and fire. Light swirls in your eyes, a rush of maddening color, of moths caught alight, and you are falling, falling. "Jesus, Robbie," comes a voice. "Are you okay? Please be okay."

XXX

My chest aches, my breath catches on a rasp like a fishhook in my throat. She looms over me, a black silhouette backlit by a starlit sky and a firelit horizon. A punk rock anthem of emergency sirens penetrates the air. I struggle to speak. "W-w-where…"

"Shhh…" she says, pressing an index finger to my lips. "Save your strength. I had to drag you out the back. You and Johnny both. The club's burning." I try to move, but realize that I'm strapped down to a gurney. She touches my face.

Her black hair, her touch, her scent. I am confused. "Where's E-Erin?"

The throbbing in my chest is suddenly overwhelmed as she digs her nails into my shoulder. "No, it's me. T... It's Terrri." She squeezes my shoulder again, tenderly this time. "Terrri Terrrors. And don't you fucking forget that, Robbie Snow." Terrri, my radiant savior in her Wonder Woman costume.

"What happened?" I ask, coughing up the words. "Oh, shit," I realize. "Christian shot me. Am I going to die?"

"No. You're good. Bullet went right through you."

"But Christian..."

"It's okay. I triggered the firepots. Kaboom. The little fucker never even knew what hit him."

"Where's Johnny? I saw him fall."

"They already loaded him into an ambulance. Christian only nicked him, but he passed out when he landed. They say he'll be okay."

"And Christian?"

"Still inside," she says, looking down. "I hope he's dead."

"I don't," I reply. "I can't. And I don't think you really do either."

She looks me in the eyes, and I know I'm right. Terrri leans in close, stroking my face. She brushes her lower lip against mine, quivering, presses her lips to mine. We kiss, our tongues probing, exploring one another's mouths to the tune of roaring flames and sirens. They try to separate us when they finally come to load me into the ambulance, but I insist that Terrri ride along.

TRACK 14
REPRISE

"You're back soon," says Terrri, climbing down from the driver's side of the van.

"Yeah, well," I say, limping along. "He doesn't do much."

"He still just sits there?" asks Terrri, helping me back up into the passenger seat. "Doesn't talk, doesn't move, doesn't do anything?"

"That's what they say," I answer, fastening my seatbelt and watching as she climbs in behind the steering wheel. "He's so damaged, so fucked up, they don't have a clue what's going on inside his head. They just try to keep him comfortable, drugged, y'know."

"Fuck," says Terrri, punctuating the expletive by turning the key and gunning the engine. "What a miserable existence."

"Yeah, I can't imagine," I say. "Still, alive has got to be better than nothing."

"I guess," she says.

I stroke the back of her hand. "I'm glad he's alive. You wouldn't want his death on your conscience."

"I guess," answers Terrri. She looks down, then back up at me. "You're right," she says.

Terrri drops the van into reverse, backing out of the parking space, moves it up into gear and we head for the exit from the hospital's parking lot. "They told me that Erin came out to see him day before yesterday."

"Oh yeah?" asks Terrri, maneuvering onto the road. "Guess it's about time."

I shrug. "Yeah, sure." I watch the road roll past through the dirty window. "Sounds like everyone was hitting her up for autographs and shit."

"No shit?"

"No shit. You'd think they'd have been cool about it, all things considered, but no." Terrri pulls onto the freeway, starting back toward our practice space.

We drive along in silence, the rumble of the van filling in for conversation. We pass a pickup truck bearing a faded Heroes for Goats sticker on the back window. "You know," I say, finally breaking the silence. "You saved my life."

"Yeah," says Terrri. "I know. Weird, isn't it? I guess it means I'm in love with you or something." She reaches out her right hand and I take it in mine.

"I guess I'm in love with you or something, too," I say, rubbing my thumb along the back of her hand, caressing it. "So what do we do about it?"

She thinks about this for a few seconds, then lifts my hand to her lips, kissing it. "We keep on rocking," says Terrri, glancing over at me. "And I guess it's your turn to save my life next time."

"It's a deal," I say, and together we drive off into the sunset.

XXX

Erin pulls on her headphones, hoping to close her eyes and shut out the world. She moves to press play, to listen to *White Light/White Heat* and hide away beneath a wash of music. But instead of pressing the button, on an impulse she doesn't fully comprehend, Erin ejects the cassette, turns it over, and replaces it into the Walkman, pausing only long enough to read the handwritten label: *The Velvet Underground Live at Max's Kansas City.*

The world moves faster now, she thinks. Might as well learn to love what's on the other side. Amid the ancient, ambient noise of crowd, hall, and tape, "I'm Waiting for the Man" begins to play.

Erin drums her fingers in time to Billy Yule's youthful pounding, conscious of a nagging emptiness within. The stand-in drummer, she thinks. *The substitute.* He's no Mo Tucker, but...

Suddenly, it dawns on Erin why *Live at Max's* always brings her down. It's not what she always believed, that the album captured a great band, maybe the greatest band of all time, right at its moment of collapse. Instead, it's the apathetic audience, chit-chatting, ordering drinks, and scoring drugs, as the band plays on, unaware that rock and roll is about to change forever. Summer, 1970: John Cale was already long gone, Lou Reed was faking it, about to quit and strike off on his own, Mo Tucker was off having babies. *Everybody moving on.*

Like me, she thinks. I've moved on. *Haven't I?* Her thoughts drift back to Christian, bandaged and blank. She thinks of that last Heroes for Goats show, of Christian's drumming, as active and energetic as the sixteen-year-old stand-in on the cassette. She thinks of Robbie Snow, playing strong then blowing it by acting like he owned her. She wonders where she'd be, where they'd all be, had she stuck around.

You know people, you do things, and then you move along, thinks Erin. Most of the time, you never see them again. You couldn't have known Christian would weird out. Erin thinks of Paulie and the band, of tomorrow's show, of seeing Candy next week. I've moved on, she thinks.

XXX

There is pain, constant, inside and out, and so you drum to pass the time, to pass those forever stretches between the rare moments of contact when they change your bandages, flood your body with the drugs you need to push back the tide. You drum because you're the drummer, the heartbeat of the band, and even though your body refuses to move, it is up to you to keep the beat alive.

In your mind's eye, you tap your sticks to lead the band in. "One, two... One, two, three, four." It's a simple rhythm, a shuffling bass drum on one and three, snare and ride alternating. The heartbeat of the band.

You take the first couple of bars alone, tight enough that the rest of the band can play along, loose enough that it swings.

The bass slides in, a walking bluesy run in C. The old one-four-five. Simple as it gets, but tricky to master. You add toms to the rhythm, glancing over at the bassist as you do so. It's Robbie Snow, plucking away at a cream-colored vintage Rickenbacker, smiling at you. All is forgiven.

At center stage, she joins your rhythm, shaking her long black hair as she strums power chords on a white pearlescent Gretsch. She leans to the mic, taking it in both of her hands. In a smoky voice, she purrs, "All right. We've had a great time playing for you tonight, but it's almost last call." She glances at a bare wrist. "So we've got one more tune for you. You don't have to go home, but you can't stay here."

The band launches into a punked-up version of Mott the Hoople's "The Golden Age of Rock 'n' Roll." It's note-perfect, with her stuttering guitar riffs covering the original's percussive, driving piano.

You reach the bridge, locking into a steady, climbing rhythm as she takes the mic stand in hand, leaning toward the crowd. "And now I'd like to introduce you all to the band," she says with a flourishing gesture. "Ninety-six decibel freaks, every one of them. On drums, Christian." You beat out a fill, twirling your sticks. "On bass," she smiles at Robbie, blowing him a kiss. "Robbie fucking Snow!"

"And I'm... Aw, you all know who I am, don't you?" She flutters her eyes. "Well, don't you?" She pauses, then snarls, "I'm the motherfuckin' Queen of Rock."

ACKNOWLEDGMENTS

To three power duos in particular, who made this book possible: Cameron and Kirsten, Carlton and Rose, and Spike and Christopher. You rock!

To cover photographer Theresa Kereakes and designer Matthew Revert, thanks for a jacket that will stand apart in the bins.

To Jennifer, my army, for lighting my path, sharing my journey, and loving me in spite of myself.

To the late Dr. Dan Plummer, for tinnitus, Jimmy Page-isms, and the old one-four-five...

...and to my parents, whose garage was Ground Zero for many misadventures.

Special thanks to Dodie Bellamy, Maxine Chernoff, and the San Francisco State University Creative Writing department.

ABOUT THE AUTHOR

Ross E. Lockhart is the managing editor of Night Shade Books. A lifelong fan of supernatural, fantastic, speculative, and weird fiction, he holds degrees in English from Sonoma State University (BA) and San Francisco State University (MA). In 2011, he edited the acclaimed anthology *The Book of Cthulhu*. A follow-up, *The Book of Cthulhu II* was published in October 2012 by Night Shade Books. He lives in an old church in Petaluma, CA, with his wife Jennifer, hundreds of books, and Elinor, who is fitting in nicely. Visit him online at www.haresrocklots.com.

LAZY FACIST 2012

The Obese by Nick Antosca
Anatomy Courses by Blake Butler and Sean Kilpatrick
A Parliament of Crows by Alan M. Clark
The Last Final Girl by Stephen Graham Jones
Zombie Bake-Off by Stephen Graham Jones
The Collected Works of Scott McClanahan Vol. I by Scott McClanahan
The Devil in Kansas by David Ohle
Frowns Need Friends Too by Sam Pink
I Am Going to Clone Myself Then Kill the Clone and Eat It by Sam Pink
No One Can Do Anything Worse to You than You Can by Sam Pink
A Pretty Mouth by Molly Tanzer
Broken Piano for President by Patrick Wensink
Everything Was Great Until It Sucked by Patrick Wensink

COMING IN 2013

The Human War Trilogy by Noah Cicero
Moon Babes of Bicycle City by Mike Daily
Zombie Sharks with Metal Teeth by Stephen Graham Jones
The Doom That Came to Lolcats by Douglas Lain
Rontel by Sam Pink
The Humble Assessment by Kris Saknussemm
Dyldoe: A Novel by Molly Tanzer
Colony Collapse by J.A. Tyler
Expletive Deleted by Patrick Wensink

Plus many more!

www.ingramcontent.com/pod-product-compliance
Lightning Source LLC
Chambersburg PA
CBHW030257270626
47156CB00022B/2927